SEALS ON THE SLED

'Listen!' Mandy said urgently. The thin, wavering cry came again, weaker this time.

'It sounds like a seal,' Bart said immediately. 'Where is it, I wonder?' He cupped his hands around his face and scanned the sea.

And then Mandy spotted a tangled heap of blue fishing net lying further up the beach. She hurried over to investigate. As she drew closer, she saw that the net was moving!

'Over here!' she yelled to Bart. She got down on her knees, her heart hammering. Four large black eyes peered back at her. A pair of whiskery muzzles twitched in alarm. Two young seals were trapped in the netting. They squirmed about, paddling small flippers, fighting for their freedom.

Pity flowed through Mandy. 'Oh, Bart!' she gasped. 'How awful. We must get them out of here – quickly!'

Animal Ark series

LUCY DANIELS

Seals
— on the —
Sled

Illustrations by Ann Baum

**Hodder
Children's
Books**

a division of Hodder Headline Limited

Special thanks to Ingrid Maitland

**Thanks also to C. J. Hall, B.Vet.Med., M.R.C.V.S., for reviewing
the veterinary information contained in this book.**

Animal Ark is a trademark of Working Partners Limited
Text copyright © 2002 Working Partners Limited
Created by Working Partners Limited, London W6 0QT
Original series created by Ben M. Baglio
Illustrations copyright © 2002 Ann Baum

First published in Great Britain in 2002
by Hodder Children's Books

For more information about Animal Ark,
please contact www.animalark.co.uk

10 9 8 7 6 5 4 3 2 1

A Catalogue record for this book is available from the British
Library

ISBN 0 340 79553 0

Typeset by Avon Dataset Ltd, Bidford-on-Avon, Warks

Printed and bound in Great Britain by
Clays Ltd, St Ives plc

Hodder Children's Books
a division of Hodder Headline Limited
338 Euston Road
London NW1 3BH

One

'At last!' Mandy Hope cried excitedly, as the taxi drew up at the edge of the dock. She craned her neck at the looming hull of the boat, moored in the harbour waters of Goose Bay. All around was a flurry of activity. Crane drivers swung their cargo aboard the deck and men in hard hats scurried up and down the gangplank.

Mandy got out of the taxi and examined the boat more carefully. It was a coastal freighter, and its job was to serve the rugged coastline of Labrador, northern Canada, transporting freight and passengers to and from the little town of Nain.

Rust scarred the peeling white paint of the boat, but Mandy thought it was wonderful. She could hardly wait to get aboard.

'*Northern Ranger*,' she read aloud, as her father paid the taxi driver and began unloading their bags.

'This is her last journey of the year,' said Emily Hope, Mandy's mum. 'Soon it will be too icy for her to sail. I expect that's why it's so busy.'

A long line of people was shuffling slowly up the gangplank, weighed down with bags and boxes of supplies. Mandy knew this was because they would be sailing to towns far north along the coast, where the spreading ice was about to cut them off until the spring thaw. It was only mid-November but already she could see islands of thick ice on the water in the harbour. Brittle chunks of it bobbed about, knocking hollowly against the hull of the boat.

'Right,' said Adam Hope, a suitcase in each hand. 'Shall we go aboard?'

Mandy followed her mum up the gangplank. Above her, seabirds screamed and the smell of oil and salt was strong in the air. She felt a million miles away from her home in Welford, Yorkshire, where her parents owned and ran Animal Ark, a busy veterinary surgery. During their absence, a locum vet would manage Animal Ark, while Mr and Mrs Hope researched environmental impact on sub-arctic wildlife on behalf of a Canadian university.

The boat was warm, a welcome contrast to the bitterly cold day. Mr Hope showed his ticket and managed to get directions to their cabin. In single file, they made their way down one flight of steps, then another, and along a gangway. The narrow passage was dimly lit. Mandy pressed herself up against the wall to allow other passengers to pass by.

'Have you found our cabin, Adam?' Mrs Hope called out, raising her voice to be heard above the noise of clattering boots and people shouting. Her long auburn hair had come tumbling free of its clasp. She clutched their laptop computer to her chest.

'Right here,' puffed Mr Hope, as he opened the door.

Mandy stepped inside. 'Wow!' she cried. 'It's great!'

It was a four-berth cabin, with two bunk beds. Mandy immediately claimed the upper bunk with a porthole at its end. She opened one door to reveal a narrow wardrobe, and then examined the tiny bathroom. 'There's even a tooth mug!' she exclaimed happily.

'We couldn't be cosier,' smiled her mother.

'Cramped, but fun,' grinned Adam Hope. He switched on the desk-lamp and sank into a comfortable looking armchair.

Mrs Hope unzipped their bags and began hanging a few items in the narrow cupboard.

'Can I go and explore?' asked Mandy. It was wonderful to be on her feet and active again, after their long flight to Goose Bay from Churchill, in the province of Manitoba. They'd spent ten days in Churchill where Mandy had helped to care for a polar bear cub that had become separated from his mother. Now, they would have just one night aboard the *Northern Ranger* before arriving in Nain, where they planned to spend a week with the Bailey family. Adam and Emily Hope had never met the family before but Mrs Bailey worked at the Wildlife Research Station where Adam and Emily would be basing themselves during their stay. Mandy had been told that the Baileys had a son who was twelve and an animal lover like herself. She was looking forward to meeting him but, first, there was the boat trip to enjoy.

'Take care, Mandy,' Mrs Hope said. 'They're loading heavy freight.'

'I will.' Mandy made a mental note of their cabin number and set off up the gangway.

The last of the passengers had boarded and the crew was closing the boat's doors. She followed her nose to a cafeteria, where already the scent of something delicious was beginning to waft around the tables and chairs. There was an open door leading to a deck and she ventured out, gasping in the sudden cold.

The blast from the horn made Mandy jump. It was the signal that the *Northern Ranger* was on its way. The engines began to shudder and the freighter eased away from the dock.

'*There* you are,' said Mandy's dad, joining her at the rail.

Emily Hope was right behind him. 'Gosh, it's cold out here!' she said, fastening the top button of her duffle coat.

'Did you know that the stretch of coast we're going to be sailing along is known as Iceberg Alley?' Adam Hope asked.

'I hope we see an iceberg,' Mandy said eagerly.

'We're bound to. They drift down from the Arctic at this time of the year, so they're all over the place,' her dad said.

'Well, let's hope the *Northern Ranger* stays clear of them,' smiled Mrs Hope. 'Icebergs can be very dangerous. Most of their bulk is hidden below the water. In fog, or at night, ships can collide with them and split apart.'

'Yikes!' said Mandy, pulling a face. She shivered at the thought of being tossed into the freezing water in the dead of night.

The bow of the freighter pointed due east and she set out at a lumbering pace along the Hamilton Inlet, bound for the coast, and her northward voyage to Nain.

Mandy felt someone come up to the rail beside her. She turned to see an elderly man, his tanned face lined with the signs of age and an outdoor life. Mandy smiled at him and stepped aside to make room.

'Thank you,' said the old man, resting his gloved hands on the rail. 'Where are you travelling to?'

'Nain,' Mandy replied.

'That's an unusual place for a holiday!' said the man.

'Actually, my husband and I are going to be working there,' Emily Hope put in. 'We'll be based at the Wildlife Research Station.'

'I live in Nain,' the man told them with a smile. 'I know the Station.' He explained that he was a retired fisherman, travelling home after a visit to the island of Newfoundland. He'd been to stock up on food for the coming winter.

'Food?' Mandy echoed, puzzled. 'Aren't there any shops in Nain?'

'A few stores, yes,' the old man nodded. 'But it's very expensive to buy there because all supplies have to be flown in. In the summer, before the ice comes, supplies arrive by boat. Then everything is much cheaper.'

'Why do people live in such an isolated place?' Mandy asked.

'Fishing,' he told her. 'It's a big industry around here. And there's a big nickel mine at Voisey's Bay.' Suddenly he turned to Mandy and grinned, his brown eyes gleaming like shiny pebbles. 'Do you like whales?' he asked.

'Oh, yes!' she said.

'Then you could be in luck tomorrow.' He winked. 'Look to the east. You might see humpback whales, journeying south for the winter.'

Mandy beamed. Tomorrow she would begin to get to know this remote part of the world, and the creatures that made it their home. But, for now, she was looking forward to being rocked to sleep in her narrow bunk bed in their cabin below.

At some time in the night, the *Northern Ranger* had left behind the Hamilton Inlet. Mandy peered from her porthole in the pale light of early morning and saw they were out on the open sea. Salty spray lashed the thick glass of the round pane and the boat pitched and rolled. Mandy lay on her front, looking out, listening to the creaks as the vessel strained against the water.

Beneath her, Adam Hope snored softly, but her mother was awake, reading. Mandy climbed down the ladder attached to the side of the bunk. 'I want to go on deck and see if I can spot any whales,' she whispered.

'Put on your warmest things,' Mrs Hope advised. 'Be careful.'

In spite of the early hour, there was quite a gathering on deck. Among them was the old fisherman she had spoken with the evening before. Mandy soon understood the reason for the excited chatter. A pod of humpback whales was cruising the waters to the east of the boat.

'There!' The old man pointed, as soon as he spotted Mandy. 'See them?'

Mandy hurried to the railing and peered out. She saw a smooth, grey flipper, waving from the ocean. A second, smaller humpback was lying on the surface on its side, its jaws open.

'Oh, wow!' Mandy cried, and her voice was snatched by an icy wind. She gripped the wooden handrail tightly, tasting salt on her tongue. 'They're amazing!'

'It's the only whale to have such long flippers – over a metre in length,' said her friend, his voice raised against the noise of the wind and the sea.

The sight of the whale captivated Mandy. As she watched, it arched its back and dived into the waves. She saw its curved lower back and finally the fluke, or tail, raised vertically as the huge animal disappeared beneath the water.

'Have we missed anything?' Adam Hope arrived

at the railing, his arm linked with Mandy's mum's.

'Oh, Dad! There was a great humpback whale!' Mandy exclaimed. 'You just missed him!'

But there were more whales to come, and the passengers on the *Northern Ranger* were treated to a pantomime of play by a small pod on their way south. A few of the younger animals broke through the surface, their flippers slapping the surface of the water like drumbeats.

'Where will they go?' Mandy asked wistfully, wishing the whales would stay.

'To where the sea is warmer,' said the old man. 'The grey whale goes as far south as California and Mexico, the longest migration made by any mammal in the world.'

'They're remarkable,' Adam Hope said, lowering his binoculars as the last of the whales sank out of sight.

'What a treat,' Mrs Hope smiled. 'And now, let's find some breakfast!'

From the portholes in the cafeteria, Mandy could see the thin ribbon of land on the horizon. The *Northern Ranger* headed for port, as the weather worsened. Mandy had to make a grab for her glass when the boat listed to one side. She pushed her plate away from her, suddenly feeling unwell.

'Let's go on deck,' Emily Hope suggested. 'You need some fresh air.'

As Mandy took in great gulps of the freezing air, she had her first sighting of the icebergs she had been longing to see. They rose out of the sea in spectacular geometric shapes, dazzling white or glassy blue from the reflection of the water.

'They're so . . . graceful!' Mandy enthused. 'Huge . . .'

'Awe-inspiring,' said Mr Hope.

Emily Hope folded her arms tightly around her. 'It's got colder, Adam,' she remarked. 'There's a huge amount of ice floating in the sea.'

'There's certainly more ice than usual for this time of year,' a fellow passenger agreed.

'Really?' Mandy looked at the woman holding on to the railing. She seemed concerned.

'Yes.' The woman nodded, frowning. 'I make this journey every year, and I've not seen the ocean quite so filled with pack ice as it is now.'

'Will the captain put into port, do you think?' Adam Hope asked.

'I doubt it,' she replied. 'We have to get through

– there's no other way for the local people to get home.'

'I'm sure we'll make it!' Emily Hope slipped an arm around Mandy's shoulders. Her nose was bright red with the cold.

They watched the boat pulling into dock to unload freight for the inhabitants of Makkovik. As the big cranes began to pluck the cargo from the deck, the Hopes headed back inside for some warming hot chocolate. Mandy was feeling much better after a spell outside.

From Makkovik, they called at the tiny communities of Postville and Hopedale. The sleek, dark bodies of basking seals dotted the rocky shore as they motored through the choppy water, hugging the coastline. A few gleaming heads bobbed in the water.

Mandy was entranced. 'Look, Dad! Mum!' She pointed, her eyes wide.

'They're Harp seals,' said Emily Hope.

'Why are they called that?' Mandy asked.

'Because of the dark markings on the bodies of the adult seals,' Mr Hope explained. 'People say the pattern looks like a harp.'

'I wish we could see them close up,' Mandy said.

With the lumbering approach of the noisy boat, the seals had begun to slither away into the water.

'They should be migrating south round about now,' Emily Hope said, passing Mandy her binoculars. 'Their breeding ground is in the Strait of Belle Isle, far to the south of Goose Bay, between Labrador and Newfoundland.'

'So, they're swimming in the opposite direction to where we're going?' Mandy said.

'That's right,' Mrs Hope confirmed.

'Did you know that Harp seals sing when they're underwater?' Mandy's dad said.

'You mean like dolphins?' Mandy asked.

'That's right. Apparently it's quite tuneful – to other Harp seals, at least!' Adam Hope joked.

'Do they make that noise on land, too?' asked Mandy.

'No, not exactly,' Emily Hope put in. 'It's just a bark, or a whinny, you'll hear on land. You have to go deep sea diving to hear them sing.'

Mandy shuddered, peering into the icy sea. 'I wouldn't fancy that today!' she laughed.

Strong wind and sleet followed the boat on her journey up the coast and she pitched and tossed on the choppy water. Standing on deck, Mandy became colder and colder, and she reminded herself that she was deep in the sub-arctic, not far from the Arctic Circle itself. Suddenly, a vast iceberg appeared up ahead.

'Iceberg!' Mandy tugged at her father's sleeve. 'Oh! Wow!'

The ice mountain was carved into towering peaks and ridges. It soared above the highest point of the boat. Several chunks had broken away and bobbed on the surface of the sea.

'What a sight!' Adam Hope enthused, adjusting the lens of his camera. The ice seemed to be thickening, floating in smooth, thick plains as far as Mandy could see.

'I can see why this is the *Northern Ranger's* last trip this year,' Mandy said quietly. She wondered how the captain was going to navigate a path through the treacherous looking ice.

She shivered and her mother suggested they go inside to warm up. They had just stepped into the cafeteria, when the boat's engines began to strain. Mandy heard a powerful grinding noise and felt the deck shuddering beneath her feet.

'What's going on?' Mr Hope wondered aloud. He staggered against Mandy as the vessel lurched, and she in turn bumped into her mother. Emily Hope steadied herself against a table. People began to rush to the windows to look out. There was a babble of raised voices.

'Pack ice!' someone shouted.

Mandy squeezed her way to the window. The boat had stopped, but the engines still throbbed. A great sheet of ice lay pressed alongside her hull.

Then a voice came crackling over the intercom, and a hush fell in the room.

'This is Captain Dan Foley speaking. I've got bad news, folks. We've hit a stretch of ice. We're stuck!'

Two

'Stuck!' Mandy echoed, wide-eyed. She backed away from the window. 'Wow! Mum, Dad, look at this *ice*! The boat has crunched right into it!'

Mr and Mrs Hope had found their own spaces at the window. All around them people were peering out, shaking their heads and muttering.

A crew member was making his way through the crowd in the cafeteria.

'Ladies and gentlemen,' he began, 'we are not in any danger, so please don't be alarmed. At this moment, an icebreaker ship is on its way to help us.'

'Why don't we get out of this crush and go on deck? We can watch for its arrival,' Emily Hope suggested.

'Good idea!' Mandy scrambled for the door, zipping up her coat as she went.

The ice imprisoning the boat creaked and groaned like a living thing. In places it had folded into itself, erupting from the ocean and overlapping in thick wedges like cracked icing on a Christmas cake.

Once outside, it was clear why the ship couldn't move. The metre-thick ice had closed tightly around the *Northern Ranger*. They were well and truly trapped. There was nothing for it but to wait for rescue.

Mandy looked around her at the staggering scene. In the distance, she could see a few dozen small brown specks, like leaves that had fallen from a tree. 'More Harp seals!' She pointed them out to her parents.

As she watched, fascinated, a pair of sleek, dark grey bodies suddenly appeared on the shelf of ice that imprisoned the ship. Lifting their noses, they sniffed cautiously and flopped a bit nearer. Now they were close enough for Mandy to see their shiny black noses and long whiskers. Their bright, liquid eyes regarded the ship curiously. Then, alarmed by the shouts of the crew, they plunged quickly from the ice back into the sea.

Mandy felt as though she could have watched the seals forever. 'They're gorgeous,' she breathed. Then her attention was drawn by the arrival of the icebreaker.

'Here comes our rescuer!' Mrs Hope said.

'But it looks like an ordinary boat,' Mandy remarked.

'Actually, it's specially designed with a reinforced bow and very powerful engines, so it can cut through the pack ice,' her mum explained.

The ship was making its way towards the stranded *Northern Ranger* at quite a speed. As it drew closer, Mandy could hear the ice splitting and cracking in its path.

'It must be very strong,' she said. She noticed the old fisherman had come up to join her.

'Some of the icebreaker ships are equipped with compressors, which shoot streams of air bubbles under the hull. It helps to make sure that the metal hull doesn't stick to the ice,' he told her. 'It is very powerful.'

'So it will break through the ice right away?' she asked him hopefully.

'We can't be certain of that,' the old man said, shaking his head. 'We'll just have to hope for the best.'

Mandy saw her mum and dad exchange glances. What would happen if the icebreaker failed to free them from the grip of the pack ice? Mandy knew that the icebergs around them were on the move – some as high as twenty-storey buildings – and their underwater edges were as sharp as swords. It was a chilling thought.

They had a perfect view of the approaching ship. Mandy watched it as it rode up on to the pack ice, then bore down on it, crushing it. At one point, the ship reversed, then rammed forward again. Mandy was relieved to see it successfully cutting through the ice. Diesel fumes hung in the air and the *Northern Ranger* shuddered.

'We're going to be late into port,' Emily Hope said, glancing at her watch. 'I hope the Baileys won't be worried.'

'I expect they'll wait for us,' Adam Hope said.

'What'll happen if the boat can't cut us free, Dad?' Mandy asked, feeling anxious.

'It looks like it's doing a great job to me, love.' Adam Hope pointed to the plunging hull of the sturdy little icebreaker. 'But they could always airlift the passengers off the freighter, I guess.'

'I'd rather get there by boat,' Mandy muttered. She watched the powerful icebreaker carve through the pack ice. Again and again it rammed the brittle surface, sending ice chips flying. Finally, it carved out a channel of clear water through to the open sea and soon after, the *Northern Ranger's* engines began to throb once more. A cheer went up from the people on deck. Mandy saw the captain of the icebreaker raise his cap as his ship began to turn, heading back the way it had come.

'Thank heavens for that,' said Mrs Hope, breathing a sigh of relief.

'Is it on its way to another rescue, do you think?' Mandy asked.

'Maybe,' said Adam Hope, rubbing his cold nose. 'There are some places in the far north that would be completely cut off during the long winters, if it wasn't for the icebreakers bringing supplies.'

The boat began to pitch as she sailed full speed ahead, heading for Nain.

'We'd better go down to our cabin and get our things together,' Mrs Hope said. 'It won't be long before we dock.'

A fleet of fishing boats lay at anchor in the bay at Nain.

Mandy stood on deck, as their boat eased gently through the harbour entrance. 'How will we recognise the Baileys?' she asked, her eyes scanning the dock.

'They'll find us,' Mr Hope grinned. 'I sent a photograph ahead of our arrival.'

He was right. As soon as they stepped off the gangway, a small, fair-haired woman hurried forward. A fur-lined hood framed her face, but Mandy noticed her warm smile right away.

'Mrs Hope?' She put out her hand.

'Irene?' Emily Hope smiled. 'I'm Emily, and this is Mandy, my daughter, and my husband, Adam. It's nice of you to meet us.'

Mrs Bailey shook hands with Mr Hope and Mandy. 'How was your journey?' she asked.

'Exciting!' Mandy said. 'We got stuck in the pack

ice and we had to be rescued. And we saw loads of Harp seals, and even some whales. They were amazing!'

Mrs Bailey laughed. 'In that case, you're going to get along very well with my son, Bart. I can tell you're mad about animals, like he is!'

'Oh, yes,' Mandy said, grinning.

'Good.' Mrs Bailey jingled her car keys. 'Well, let's get your things into the car and we'll head over to our house.'

The road through the town of Nain was icy and lined with banks of snow. Mrs Bailey drove carefully, pointing out things of interest on the way. 'I'm looking forward to showing you around our research station,' she said. 'At the moment, we're looking at the effects of pollution on a number of species. We're gathering some fascinating data.'

'Sounds interesting,' Adam Hope said. 'It's good of you to have us to stay.'

'You're very welcome,' she smiled.

Mandy's parents began telling Mrs Bailey about the work they were doing for the university and Mandy's mind started to drift. She noticed how few people there were compared with the busy little town of Churchill, in Manitoba, where they had stayed recently. There had been tourist buses bringing camera-laden people from around the world to see Churchill's migrating polar bears. Mandy smiled as she remembered the amazing bears, especially Polo, a lost and injured cub she had helped return to the ice.

Mrs Bailey drove the car down a narrow road that descended towards the sea. She turned left along a gravel drive running parallel with the shore, and drew up outside a wooden house with shutters at the windows. Smoke curled into the air from a chimney stack. A man Mandy took to be Mr Bailey appeared at the front door.

'Welcome!' he called.

Adam and Emily Hope got out of the car and shook hands.

'Steve Bailey,' he said warmly. 'It's nice to have you with us. Come in, come in.'

There was a blazing log fire in the sitting room. Bart Bailey was sitting at a large table, bent over a notebook.

'Bart,' said his father, 'this is Mandy, and Mr and Mrs Hope.'

The boy looked up and a grin spread across his face. He was fair, like his mother, with freckles across the bridge of his nose. He stood up and came around the table to shake hands. 'Hi,' he said, and Mandy noticed his Canadian accent. 'Good to meet you.'

She liked him at once. 'Thanks for having us,' she smiled.

'Finish your homework, Bart,' said his mother, 'while I show Mandy and her parents to their rooms.'

'See you later, Mandy,' Bart said. 'I'll show you around, if you like.'

'Thanks,' Mandy replied, following Mrs Bailey out of the room.

There was a pretty grey cat curled on the bed in Mandy's room and she bounded forward to stroke it.

'That's Vivaldi,' Mrs Bailey said. 'I hope you don't mind him? He's seems to like this room.'

'I love cats!' Mandy smiled. She looked around her. Mrs Bailey fumbled with the shutters and pushed them open. Mandy drew in her breath. A vast expanse of pack ice was stretched out below her, scarred with breaks of open water.

'Wow! We're practically on the beach here!' she cried. She hurried to the window to look out. She scanned the ice for Harp seals and caught a glimpse of a few scattered basking bodies. One of them rolled luxuriously, stretching out its flippers and exposing the underside of its chin to the wintry light.

'Not quite on the beach!' Mrs Bailey laughed. 'We're on the side of a cliff, just above the bay. It's a dramatic view, isn't it?'

'It's wonderful,' breathed Mandy. 'I can't believe I can actually see Harp seals from my window!'

'We had a fierce storm recently which broke up the pack ice and drove the seals closer in to shore,' Mrs Bailey told her.

'Do you think I'll be able to get close to them?' Mandy asked, her eyes shining.

'I'm not sure,' Irene Bailey replied. 'They're on their way south, to the Straits of Belle Isle. They only stop to rest, you see, before moving on. But you may be lucky.' She turned back the bed covers and added a folded quilt, adding, 'You might need this tonight.'

'Thanks, Mrs Bailey.' Mandy was still at the

window. She was mesmerized by the great white space spreading into the distance, and the dark bodies of the seals slithering in and out of the sea.

'I'll leave you to unpack a few things. When you're ready, Bart will give you a tour, OK?'

'OK,' Mandy grinned. Her spirits soared. She couldn't wait to explore, and for a chance to see the seals up close.

'How do we get down?' Mandy asked Bart. They were standing at the top of the cliff, looking down at the shore below.

'We can't,' Bart told her. 'There are some steps, but they've been carved out of the rocky cliff face and they're covered in ice now, so it's too dangerous.'

'Oh,' said Mandy, disappointed. 'I'd love to go to the edge of the sea.'

'Tomorrow, then.' Bart tossed a pebble off the cliff. 'I'll take you down the hill that leads to the far end of the shore. On my sled.'

'Your sled!' Mandy grinned. 'Great!'

'I made it myself,' he told her. 'It's big enough for two.'

'Sounds perfect!' she said. She looked out over the ice. There was no sign of the seals she'd seen earlier. She felt a little stab of disappointment and hoped they would return. 'We saw Harp seals on our way here,' she told Bart.

'I'm sure you did! It's like a seal highway at the moment,' Bart said.

From the edge of the Baileys' garden, Mandy had a bird's eye view of the bay below. Beyond it, the great, placid ice floes rode the darkening sea's swells. Smaller chunks of ice were tossed playfully by the waves at the shoreline. There was a crunching and crashing sound as they were dragged by the tide up the stony beach.

'I can't wait to explore,' Mandy said.

'It's getting dark,' Bart said, looking at the sky.

Mandy looked at her wristwatch. It was only half past three in the afternoon but already the sky was turning a charcoal colour. In this dusky light, the ice was tinged with mauve.

'You'll have to wait till tomorrow for your Harp seals,' Bart smiled.

Bart and Mandy had just reached the door of the house, when they noticed a man coming along the drive. He was red in the face and flustered. To Mandy's surprise, she saw that he was wrestling with a large, white bird.

'Bart! Is your mother at home?' the man called out.

'Hi, Mr Ross.' Bart sounded surprised too. 'Yes, she is. What have you got there?'

'It's a snow goose in need of some help, I'm afraid,' Mr Ross said.

Mandy looked closer. Nylon fishing line trailed from the bird's beak. 'Oh! Poor thing!' she cried. 'Has it swallowed the fish hook?'

Mr Ross nodded grimly. 'I found her on the shore.' The goose shook her head and opened her beak. She tried to flap her wings but Mr Ross held her tightly under one arm. 'I don't like to disturb your mother when she's at home, but by the time I get all the way over to Dale Rogers' rescue centre, it may be too late!' he added.

'Quick,' said Bart, taking charge. 'In here.' He flung open the front door and shouted for his mother.

Mrs Bailey came hurrying out of the kitchen, a wooden spoon in her hand. 'What?' she said. She saw Mr Ross and the goose, and shook her head. 'Oh, Bill, another one?'

'Afraid so, Irene,' said Mr Ross.

'Come in here,' she said. 'I've got a couple of extra hands to help today,' she added. 'We have some visiting vets from England staying with us.'

Mandy's parents had been drawn to the room by the general commotion and the honking of the distressed goose.

'What a sad sight,' Mrs Hope said. The goose blinked, clearly frightened, and frantically tried to escape the arms that held her. She was so beautiful – snowy white with black wing tips.

Mandy was filled with pity for the bird.

'May I?' said Adam Hope, taking the goose from Mr Ross.

'Go ahead, Adam,' Mrs Bailey said.

'It's not very often that we see a snow goose in Welford,' Mr Hope added.

Emily Hope prized open the snow goose's beak and looked in. 'There are some minor lacerations to the back of the throat,' she said.

'Will you get my bag, Mandy, love?' Mr Hope asked. Mandy sprinted for the bedroom her parents shared. She was back in an instant.

Mrs Hope uncoiled a roll of thin plastic tubing from the bag. She reached for the end of the trailing fishing line and threaded it through the tube, until it was touching the bird's beak.

'Can I help?' Mandy asked.

Mr Hope lowered the bird on to a table. 'Yes, please, Mandy. You can hold her down. I don't want to have to sedate her, so, although this might be unpleasant for her, it's best done quickly.'

Bart peered over Mandy's shoulder as she reached around the goose, pinning its protesting wings to its sides. Emily Hope stretched out the beautiful, downy neck. With one hand, Mr Hope opened her beak and slowly fed the length of piping down her throat and into the goose's gizzard. The bird struggled frantically, but Mandy held her fast.

'Oh dear,' muttered Mr Ross, frowning.

'It's OK, Mr Ross,' Mandy said quickly. 'Dad knows what he's doing.'

She watched her father gently probe the innards of the goose. Then, he pulled the tube out carefully, bringing with it a fish hook and a lead weight.

'Thank you!' Mr Ross smiled. 'That was brilliant. I love birds,' he explained. 'It really upsets me to see them hurt like this.'

'We're always pleased to be able to help,' Mrs Bailey told him kindly.

The goose seemed dazed. She coughed and stood up.

'Can we set her free now?' Bart asked Mr Hope. He nodded, so Bart gently lifted the bird from the table. With Mandy in tow, he hurried to the French windows in the sitting room. Mrs Bailey unlatched them and flung them wide. Bart lifted his arms up and the goose spread her wings – and flew. It was a thrilling sight. She rose up into the icy air, then headed east, out towards the pack ice.

'Fantastic!' Mandy breathed. She and Bart watched until the bird was just a tiny speck in the sky.

'Unfortunately, my mom and I are quite used to treating injured animals here. The best bit is setting them free,' he said.

'What kind of injuries do they suffer around here?' Mandy asked, looking round in surprise at the vast empty space.

'We have a real problem with litter on our beaches here,' Bart said grimly. 'Especially fishing nets and lines left lying around for the animals to get caught up in. It's pretty dangerous.'

'That's terrible!' Mandy said heatedly, adding, 'Isn't there a veterinary surgery in the town?'

'There's a wildlife rescue centre,' Bart explained. 'But it's quite a drive from here. The beaches need cleaning up – and I'm not the only one who thinks so.'

'Thanks again,' Mr Ross called, pulling on his mittens. 'I'll leave you now.'

'Bye,' said Mandy. 'Thanks for saving the snow goose.'

When Mr Ross had gone, Mandy went to the kitchen to lay the table. She was suddenly very hungry, and tired too. It had been an eventful day and, tomorrow, she would go exploring the icy landscape with Bart, hoping for another glimpse of some seals. She could hardly wait.

Three

It was the next morning, a Saturday, and Bart and Mandy were getting ready to go sledding. Mr and Mrs Bailey had driven Mandy's parents to work at the Wildlife Research Station, promising to be home by late afternoon.

'Look, here it is,' Bart said brightly, pushing up the garage door. The sled was propped up against a wall of the garage.

'It's great!' Mandy was impressed. The bright green sled was easily big enough for the two of them. It looked a lot sturdier than the sleds back in Welford. She was keen to have a go. Bart had said they would ride the sled across the top of the cliff, then down a gentle slope for about half a mile, to the beach. Once they reached the stony shore, they would be even closer to where the Harp seals might lie, basking on the ice floes.

'What do you think our chances are? Of seeing the seals, I mean?' she asked Bart eagerly.

He laughed. 'Pretty good,' he said. 'But you should be here in the spring, when the pups are born. You'd love it. The ice is like a giant nursery, full of white fluffy seal pups.'

'I'd love to see a newborn seal. I mean a whitecoat – that's what they're called, aren't they?' Mandy said.

Bart nodded. 'That's right. They're yellowish at first, then they turn snowy white and fluffy about two days after they're born. They feed on their mother's milk, which is ten times richer than cows' milk,' he added. 'They have to grow a thick layer of blubbery fat to keep warm.'

'How does a mother seal know her own pup when there are so many of them being born in the spring at the same time?' Mandy wondered.

'They rub noses,' Bart answered. 'Each seal has its own special scent. Mother seals only have enough milk for one pup, so she can only feed her own.'

'What if she has twins?' Mandy asked.

'Twins aren't very common among Harp seals,' Bart said thoughtfully. 'But I guess she might have to share her supply between them.' Bart bent down to tie his bootlace. 'I saw a mother seal teach her pup to swim once,' he went on. 'The little thing was so fat it looked as though it was wearing a life jacket!'

Mandy laughed.

Bart straightened up and went on. 'The mother nudged the baby towards a hole in the ice – and all the time the pup squealed and squealed. Suddenly it plopped into the water, vanished for a second and then began to bob about like a little cork.'

'I'd love to see that!' Mandy smiled. 'Could it swim straight away?'

'The pups have so much fat that they can't sink,' Bart explained. 'But they have to learn to swim properly or they won't survive. They are easy prey for whales, especially around here.'

Tiny snowflakes spiralled down as Mandy looked up at the sky. It was bitterly cold. She could feel a dull ache in her toes in spite of her sturdy boots. Once they got going, she knew she would soon warm up. 'Let's go, then!' she urged Bart, pulling on her mittens.

They dragged the sled along the driveway to the gate, then crossed the narrow road, where a track led along the top of the cliff. From up here, Mandy had a bird's eye view of the Atlantic Ocean and its covering of chunky ice.

'Is it possible to walk out on to the sea ice?' she asked, swiftly scanning the floes for signs of the seals. There were no dark bodies out of the water, but here and there she spotted a head, drifting in the channels of sea between the islands of ice.

'Yes, during the winter it is,' Bart replied. 'But you have to watch out for the bobbing holes. You wouldn't want to fall into one of those!' He chuckled.

'Bobbing holes?' asked Mandy. 'What are they?'

'Smooth, round holes in the ice, made by the seals,' Bart told her. 'They dive in to fish, then pop up again when they need to breathe. Did you know they can stay under the water for an hour without coming up to breathe?'

'A whole hour? That's amazing!' she said.

'Come on,' Bart grinned. 'Let's go and see if we can spot some close up.'

He heaved the sled to the edge of the crest of the snowy hill and positioned it with its nose pointing down toward the sea. He held it steady while Mandy climbed gingerly aboard.

'Ready?' he asked.

'Ready,' said Mandy, gripping the rails on the side of the sled. Bart gave her a push. She took off down the slope, gathering speed, then came to a lurching halt when the sled cruised suddenly off to the left and she tumbled into the soft snow, laughing.

'Come on back,' he yelled.

Mandy trudged uphill, pulling the sled behind her. When she reached the top she was breathless, her cheeks pink from the cold.

'I guess we'll be better off if we both get on,' said Bart with a grin. 'We'll go along this way,' he pointed. 'We must be careful to steer around that tree over there, see it?'

Mandy nodded. 'Then where?'

'Then we'll start to go down the hill. There's a crevice to the right, which is quite deep. We don't want to fall into that!'

'Oh, no,' Mandy agreed. She wondered what her best friend, James Hunter, would say if he knew that she and Bart were using the sled as a means of transport, rather like she and James used their bicycles to get around in Welford!

The slope was deserted, and, from up here, only the roof of the Baileys' house was faintly visible. There were no other signs of life, not a plume of smoke from a distant chimney or the background crunch of car tyres on ice.

Bart sat up front, with Mandy behind him. He nudged the sled along, using the heels of his

boots. It gained momentum, getting faster and faster, until Mandy felt as though she was flying. The icy wind stung her cheeks and she gave a great whoop of joy. The sled skimmed over the earth, carving a path over the natural contours of the land.

Bart leaned this way and that, expertly guiding the big sled around the towering, snow-covered pine tree. Mandy clung to the sturdy sides of the sled, squinting against the cold and the glare of daylight on the snow.

All too soon, the ride was over, ending when the sled abruptly changed course and tipped them unceremoniously into the snow.

Mandy sat up, smiling, and brushed the loose snow off her jacket.

Bart had lost a glove and was scrabbling around trying to find it. 'Ouch! Ouch! Cold hand,' he muttered, as he hopped about.

Mandy got to her feet to help him. They had ridden all the way down the hill to where a crescent of pebbles formed a thin strip of beach, against which the iron-grey sea lapped. She heard the pack ice groan and crunch as it shifted in the currents of the sea. Great chunks of ice were drifting right up to the edges of the beach, and some were being rolled up on to the shore by the waves.

Mandy was fascinated. It was as though the approaching ice was taking the sea prisoner. 'What a great ride!' she called to Bart.

Suddenly, she heard a hoarse, low cry. Mandy spun round in the direction from which the noise had come. 'What was that?' she said, but Bart didn't hear her. He had wandered off back up the hill in search of his glove. A piercing shriek drifted across to Mandy. A gull swooped down, its wings outspread, shrieking again and, for a moment, Mandy thought she must have imagined the chilling noise. But then it came again. She darted forward and looked up and down the stony beach. The sound came again.

'Hey!' Bart yelled from the slope. 'I found my glove.' He paused, then added in a puzzled voice, 'Where did you get to, Mandy?'

'I'm behind this rock, come quickly,' Mandy shouted.

Bart bounded towards her. 'What is it?' He looked faintly alarmed.

'Listen!' Mandy said urgently. The thin,

wavering cry came again, weaker this time.

'It sounds like a seal,' Bart said immediately. 'Where is it, I wonder?' He cupped his hands around his face and scanned the sea.

And then Mandy spotted a tangled heap of blue fishing net lying further up the beach. She hurried over to investigate. As she drew closer, she saw that the net was moving!

'Over here!' she yelled to Bart. She got down on her knees, her heart hammering. Four large black eyes peered back at her. A pair of whiskery muzzles twitched in alarm. Two young seals were trapped in the netting. They squirmed about, paddling small flippers, fighting for their freedom.

Pity flowed through Mandy. 'Oh, Bart!' she gasped. 'How awful. We must get them out of here – quickly!'

Bart sank to his knees beside Mandy. 'They're Harp seal pups. Poor things.'

'Come on, help me. Quick,' Mandy urged him. She grabbed hold of the thick nylon net, but Bart stopped her.

'No,' he said. 'It's best to leave them as they are. They're very weak and dehydrated. Look, their eyes are all dry. It looks like the fishing net has sliced into them in places. If we pull it off, it might make the injuries even worse!'

Mandy's hands dropped to her sides and she studied the seals for a moment. They were a silvery grey, with darker markings across their smooth backs and faces. They had stopped struggling now and lay staring out fearfully from the net. Their big, sad eyes broke Mandy's heart. They needed help, and fast.

But Bart was carefully weighing up their options. 'Mandy,' he said gravely, 'This could be very serious. They're only pups and if they're badly dehydrated they probably don't stand a very good chance.'

'Oh, Bart,' Mandy exclaimed. 'Can't we just put them back into the sea?'

'Definitely not,' he said, slowly shaking his head. 'We mustn't take that chance. We can't free them of the net, and inside it, they might drown.'

'Oh,' Mandy said miserably. She hugged herself. She was freezing and her helplessness was making her feel desperate. They had to do something!

'Anyway, they're probably far too weak to swim or hunt or anything.' Bart walked around the seals in circles, pacing anxiously. He was frowning hard, trying to think.

'Where would their parents be?' Mandy asked suddenly, wondering if they might be close enough to help in some way.

'These seals won't be with their mothers any more, and their group will have moved on south by now,' Bart said in a desolate tone. 'These little guys must have been left behind.'

'What can we do?' Mandy pleaded. 'Shall I go for help?' She knew she had to be guided by Bart. His experience with arctic animals was much greater than hers.

Bart shook his head. 'There's nobody around who could help. We need to get them home as fast as we can.'

'Right,' Mandy said eagerly. She stood up and the seals shrank away, cowering down inside the net in terror at her sudden movement. 'Tell me what to do.'

'Our best chance of saving them is to get them to the house for treatment,' Bart explained. 'But they'll be too heavy for us to carry. I don't want to risk dragging them along in the net either.' He looked really worried.

Mandy looked down at the seals with a heavy heart. What on earth could they do? Then, out of the corner of her eye, she spotted Bart's sled at the edge of the beach. 'What about your sled?' she cried. 'We can pull them up the hill on that – that way we can keep them wrapped in the net!'

'Hey! That's a great idea,' Bart said approvingly.

Mandy looked down at the two small faces, pressed up against the net. They seemed completely exhausted. Slowly, she approached the netting and eased her finger through the mesh. She made contact with the silky grey coat of the bigger seal and stroked it gently. The bewildered animal twisted its head and gazed at her with its huge, pleading eyes. She heard a soft whimper.

'We're going to help you,' Mandy whispered. 'You're going to be all right.'

'Careful.' Bart spoke warningly. 'Seals have a nasty bite, though it does look as if these two are too worn out to be aggressive.'

Mandy stood up. 'Right,' she said. 'Come on, Bart. Let's get going!' She turned and ran back to the base of the slope, where the green sled lay upside down. A frosting of light snow had coated its base. When she returned, Bart was bending over the seals, trying to assess how badly they had been injured by the net. He eased the sled as close to the seals as he could. The bigger of the two pups rolled its eyes, and barked in alarm.

'We won't hurt you,' Mandy said softly. 'We're trying to help.' But the pups were clearly terrified. Mandy took up a handful of net covering one of the seal's flippers.

'Don't get too close to their mouths,' Bart reminded her, 'just in case they do bite.'

Mandy nodded and bunched the net in her fist, gaining a sturdy grip. Bart, at the other end, did the same. Mandy knew that it was important to lift the seals as gently as they possibly could. The last thing they wanted was to cause the animals any more distress – or pain.

'One, two, three, lift!' Bart instructed. 'Gently does it.'

It took all of Mandy's strength to raise the seals. Frightened, they began to whimper and squirm about, making it all the more difficult.

Mandy lowered the net back down on to the ground, breathless. 'They're so heavy!' she gasped. 'I'm not sure I can manage.'

Bart let go of the netting. 'I've got an idea,' he

said. 'Let's build a ramp out of the snow. That way we'll be able to slide them up along it, and on to the sled.'

'Good idea!' Mandy agreed. Quickly, they used the sides of their snow boots to drag together a heap of snow, patting it into a smooth sloping ramp with their hands.

'OK,' Mandy muttered, standing up. 'Now, let's try to slide them on to the sled.'

They stood side by side at one end of the bunched netting. On the count of three, they began to pull steadily. The seals slipped over the snow and up the ramp, landing with a tiny jolt on its wooden base. A cacophony of barking and whimpering broke out.

Mandy's heart went out to the two petrified pups. 'I'm so sorry,' she whispered. 'You'll soon be free. I promise.'

Bart straightened, puffing. 'There! We did it.'

Together, they gathered the trailing fishing net and tucked it around the seals. The seals whipped their heads around, following Mandy and Bart with their eyes, showing their small, sharp teeth.

'Now we'll have to get them up the hill!' Bart said. He looked along the beach. 'Let's walk along the shore for a bit before we start to climb up. The slope isn't so steep over at that end.'

'OK,' Mandy replied. She glanced up at the crest of the slope. It did seem a long, hard climb from where she was standing, but she was determined to get the young seals to safety. 'Let's go,' she said. She looked at the pups, lying side by side on the sled. One of them had closed its eyes and Mandy felt a stab of anxiety. She could see swollen, messy cuts in their skin. Would they make it back in time?

Bart handed her one side of the rope, which was attached in a loop to the front of the sled. 'Pull as hard as you can,' he advised grimly. 'I don't think we've got much time.'

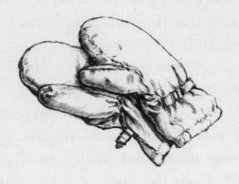

Four

Bart took hold of the other side of the rope, wrapping it around his right wrist to gain a better grip, his back to the seals on the sled. Mandy walked next to him, using both hands and all of her strength. She was glad that the settling snow had covered the beach, giving the seals a smoother ride. It would have been almost impossible to pull them along on a bare, stony shore.

The pups began their mournful squealing as soon as they set off, sending a shiver up Mandy's spine. She tried to blot it out, and focus on the importance of getting the seals back to the house. 'How do you think the seals got caught in the net, Bart?' she asked.

'Fishermen sometimes leave their nets to dry on the beach,' he replied. 'The tide takes them, and then they wash ashore some place along the coast.' He paused to take a breath. Mandy was grateful for a brief rest. 'Or they cut them adrift from the fishing boats out to sea, and leave them to float ashore. We had really strong winds a week or so ago. Maybe these guys were swept into a drifting net, then up on to the beach.'

'Can't the fishermen be stopped from being so careless?' Mandy demanded.

'Not really,' Bart said. 'There's no law or anything.'

'But these seal pups would have starved to death if we hadn't come along when we did!' Mandy was indignant.

'Probably,' he agreed, his face grim.

'What'll we feed them on, when we get them back?' Mandy asked Bart.

'I'm not sure what we've got,' he admitted. 'I guess my mom will have some kind of fish in the icebox. They eat herring, and squid, and some shellfish.'

'You said they were only pups,' Mandy reminded him. 'Does that mean they'll need milk?'

'No.' Bart shook his head and his fur-lined hood fell back. 'Harp seals are weaned when they're only two weeks old,' he explained. 'These are known as beaters. That means they are fully grown – I guess about eight months or so – but not able to swim as well as older seals.'

Mandy noted with relief that the seals were calmer now. The pair seemed suddenly resigned to this strange journey and lay slumped on the sled, looking warily around them. From time to time, the bigger of the two pups lifted its nose in the direction of the ocean. Mandy was filled with a quick sadness. She wished it were possible just to rip open the net and let the poor things go. But Bart had been right. The seals were far too weak to fend for themselves. Mandy pulled on the rope with renewed energy.

'This is where we can leave the beach and start going up the hill,' Bart said. He paused and pointed. 'Look, it's a much gentler slope than the one we came down on the sled.'

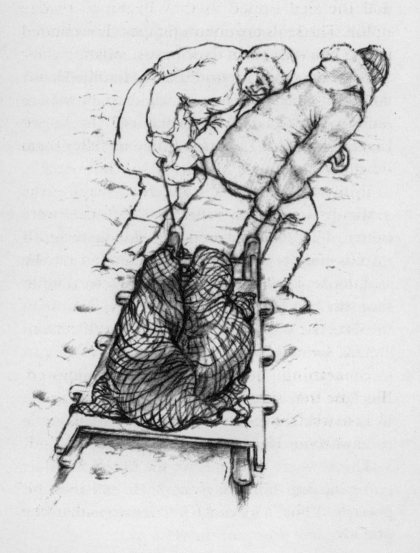

'Yes, OK,' Mandy panted. She changed course and the sled tipped as they began to trudge uphill. The seals began to whimper. They butted at the net with their dark heads, twisting their necks and looking around them balefully. Mandy could only imagine how bewildered they were feeling. It was snowing harder, and she hoped that the worsening weather would not slow them down too much.

To lift her spirits, she tried to imagine the seal pups swimming in the sea when they were better. They would launch themselves happily into the depths of the water, as swift as arrows, singing to each other in celebration of their freedom.

'Bart,' she puffed. 'Let's give the seals names.'

'OK,' he said. 'What?'

'Something musical,' Mandy suggested. 'Because they sing underwater.'

'Like what?' Bart prompted.

'How about Harmony . . . and Melody!' Mandy said.

'Yeah,' Bart agreed, glancing at her over his shoulder. 'That's nice. We'll call the smaller one Melody.'

'All right,' Mandy agreed.

'It's strange that they don't ever sing on land, isn't it?' Bart said. 'Only under the water. Nobody really knows why.'

They fell silent. Mandy sensed that Bart was as worried as she was about the seals. She kept turning around to check on them, as they slowly climbed the hill. Mandy was glad her mittens protected her hands from the rope. She had wound it tight about her palm and was pulling as hard as she could.

Each time one of the seals barked or cried out, Mandy's heart missed a beat. She was getting tired and she knew that Bart was doing most of the work hauling their heavy load. The last stages of the journey seemed painfully slow. The sled juddered and swayed as they dragged it along, trying to avoid the jutting rocks in their path and the roots of trees under the snow. At last the narrow road that ran alongside the Baileys' home was in sight and Mandy breathed a huge sigh of relief.

She checked the seals again. The smaller one was resting its head on the back of its companion. Its eyes were closed. Mandy felt icy fingers close around her heart. She wasn't even certain it was still alive.

The sled shot across the smooth surface of the road and on to the snowy driveway. Mandy looked at her watch. It was only half-past two, but maybe, just maybe, her parents or the Baileys might have returned to the house. She yelled out. 'Dad! Mum! Mrs Bailey!'

Bart dropped the rope and ran towards the front door. 'I can't see the car,' he called. 'I'm sure they're not back yet.'

'Oh, please,' Mandy muttered, crossing her fingers. 'Please be home!' She knew the young seals needed expert medical attention – and soon. She couldn't bear it if the two little seals died now, especially after the desperate journey they had made to try and save them. She waited while Bart fumbled with his key and flung open the door.

'Mom!' she heard him bellow. One of the seals coughed and squealed. Mandy could offer them no comfort at all. It was agony. And then, Bart appeared on the step at the door.

'There's nobody here, Mandy. I'm sure they're not going to be back for a while yet,' he said. He was still out of breath. 'We'll have to do what we can for the seals on our own. Let's get them out of the net, and try and feed them. It's all we can do . . .'

Five

Mandy's heart sank. But they must not give up! The pups were critically ill, but she was determined they were not going to die. With Bart's help, she would manage somehow.

'OK,' she said. 'Will you ring your mum, Bart? Tell her what's happened and ask them to come back straight away.'

'Right,' said Bart, spinning around and making for the telephone in the hall.

Mandy was left in the driveway, with the seals. The bigger of the two, Harmony, had begun butting the fishing net with its head again. Mandy took this as a good sign. At least one of them still had enough energy to struggle for freedom.

She looked around her. To the side of the house, she noticed a small closed-in area. It had four sturdy, stone walls but no roof. Mandy ran to inspect it, just as Bart came out of the house.

'I spoke to my mother,' he told her. 'They're on their way home now.'

'Good.' Mandy managed a smile. 'What's this for?' She peered in around the opening in the wall. The floor of the enclosure was concrete.

'We used to store coal there,' Bart answered. 'But mostly we use diesel now. Do you think we should unload the seals in here?'

'Yes.' Mandy nodded, her eyes shining. 'It's a perfect place! All we have to do is find something to block off this opening, so they don't get out.'

'I'll go and hunt around for something,' Bart said.

'Hurry, Bart, then we can get them off the sled,' Mandy urged him. She was longing to set the seals free from the netting.

While Bart went off in search of something to use as a makeshift door, Mandy ran to pick up a few garden tools that had been left propped up against the far wall of the bunker. There was an oilcan and funnel, and a few ceramic plant pots, too. She gathered these and stacked them outside. The bunker was a good place for the seals. They would be safe within the walls, yet still get plenty of fresh air.

Bart returned dragging a large rectangle of hardwood. 'This'll do,' he gasped. 'It's heavy enough. My dad was going to use it for shelving.'

'Great,' Mandy enthused, running to help him. 'We'll have to make sure we keep the seals barricaded inside.'

'Yes.' Bart nodded gravely. 'There are wolves around, you know. People in the town occasionally spot one lurking about.'

'Would a wolf attack a seal?' Mandy asked.

'Sure!' he said. 'A hungry wolf will eat just about anything.'

Bart found a broom and began sweeping away the debris left in the bunker.

'That's great,' Mandy called. 'They should be fine in here.'

As she walked back to the sled, Mandy silently hoped they were doing the right thing for the seals. All they could do was turn them loose into

a safe environment, and hope that her mum and
dad and the Baileys arrived in time to rehydrate
the exhausted pups. Silently, Mandy willed Mrs
Bailey and her parents to hurry. She knew from
watching her mum and dad work at Animal Ark
that rehydration was far more complicated than
just providing water for a sick animal. It meant
using a stomach tube and glucose salts.

'Hello,' she said softly, as she approached the
seals. One gave a mournful whinny.

'I know,' Mandy said sympathetically. 'You're fed
up of being stuck on the sled, and I don't blame
you.'

'Here,' said Bart, coming up behind her and
handing her the rope. 'Let's pull them over to the
bunker.'

The sled glided easily up to the entrance, and
Bart pulled it inside with Mandy heaving from
behind. The seals barked and squirmed about
while Mandy scrambled around the sled to pull
the wooden barricade into place. Bart opened his
penknife.

'You'll be careful?' Mandy couldn't help asking.

'Of course,' he said gently, and got down on
one knee. Four big, black eyes looked up as he

hovered over them. The seals seemed to sense that they were being helped, and lay still. The blade began sawing through the nylon mesh of the net. It fell away from the head of the bigger seal, like a veil. The seal shook itself, sending a shower of icy droplets over Mandy. She eased out the tangled netting, keeping a wary eye on the seal, who had begun to make a hissing sound.

Bart began to cut the net in a straight line above the seal's back. Harmony twisted his head to see what was going on. 'Watch out that it doesn't give you a nip,' Bart said to Mandy. 'Those teeth are razor sharp.'

Mandy nodded. 'I'll be careful,' she promised.

Bart snipped away, shifting from knee to knee on the hard, cold concrete floor.

'Let me have a go,' Mandy offered.

'No, it's OK. I'm nearly done,' he replied.

At last the net lay in piles on the floor around the sled. As Mandy tugged the net from under Harmony's foreflippers, the seal launched itself forward and plopped on to the concrete.

'OK, let's give it some room,' muttered Bart. He scrambled back and stood against the makeshift door. The seal regarded him with grave, dark eyes. It shook itself again, then took a rasping, weary breath. But it didn't seem inclined to attack its human rescuers.

'Now for the other one.' Bart lifted the second seal on to the ground and peeled the fishing net back from its body. It raised its head and looked around, but stayed where it was. With a shock, Mandy realised that some of the net was stuck to Melody's sides, reaching into the flesh wounds caused by the sharp, nylon netting.

'Oh, no!' she breathed. 'That must be painful.'

'Better leave it,' Bart suggested. 'My mom will be home in a minute. I don't like the thought of ripping the net away from those wounds.'

'You're right,' Mandy said anxiously, bending forward to get a better look at Melody's injuries.

The seal rolled its eyes and opened its mouth noiselessly. Then it slumped over on to its side.

'Oh, no!' Mandy breathed. 'Is it . . .?'

'No,' Bart said quickly. 'It's alive. It's breathing, see?'

'Yes. Thank goodness.'

Bart stood up and tiptoed around Harmony and Melody, peering at them. 'They're both girls,' he announced.

Mandy nodded. 'They'll need food,' she said, trying to think carefully. 'But I'm sure they'll have to be rehydrated before they can be fed. I know that's important.'

'Let's go and have a look in the freezer, just to see if we have anything for them,' suggested Bart. 'That way, we can be ready when my mom gets home. Any fish she has might need thawing out if it's in the freezer.'

'Can we leave them, do you think?' Mandy wondered. Melody was still partially wrapped in the blue net, lying on her side, taking laboured, rasping breaths.

'I think so.' Bart lifted the sled. He slid open the door. 'Ready?'

'Ready,' said Mandy. She slipped outside and Bart shut the door quickly behind him. Then he propped it closed with a heavy stone.

'I don't think they'll have the strength to try and escape,' Mandy observed miserably, as they made for the house.

Mrs Bailey's icebox was very full. Rummaging about, Bart found several kilos of herring and pulled them out triumphantly. They prised the frozen fish apart and laid them on plates to defrost.

Then Bart ripped open a packet of chocolate biscuits, which he offered to Mandy. They had missed lunch, and she was starving. She munched her biscuit while mashing up a bit of the herring.

'Right,' she said. 'At least we'll be ready when *they* are able to eat. Let's go and see how they're doing out there.'

* * *

Melody was still slumped exactly where they had left her. Now, Harmony too, seemed sluggish and weak, as if the difficult journey up from the beach had sapped her remaining strength.

'Do you think we should try and feed them?' Bart said. 'I know they're dehydrated, but it looks like they're fading fast. Maybe the moisture in the fish might help.'

'I suppose it's worth a try,' Mandy said. 'We've got to do something!' She crouched down in a corner of the shed and dipped her hand into the bucket of herring. Choosing a small chunk, she tossed it across the floor, where it fell with a small splat beside Melody's nose. The sick pup raised her head, sniffed at the food, then lay down again.

'She doesn't want it,' whispered Bart. 'Try Harmony.'

Mandy threw a bit of herring to the bigger seal but she showed little interest in it. Mandy felt a pang of fear. She began to suspect that the seals were sicker than she had guessed.

And then, she heard a welcome sound – the voice of her father.

Bart stood up and pushed the barricade aside.

'Quick, Mr Hope, Mom . . .' he called. 'In the bunker! This way!'

'We've found some Harp seals,' Mandy blurted out, standing up and waving frantically over the wall of the bunker. 'They were trapped in some netting on the beach.'

Adam Hope raced across the drive, dragged aside the board blocking the doorway and hurried into the bunker. Mandy's mum was hard on his heels. Mrs Bailey was scrambling out of the truck.

Mandy crouched against the wall beside Melody. The bunker felt suddenly crowded with padded jackets and woolly hats. Adam and Emily Hope sank to their knees beside the weakened seals.

'Oh, goodness, Mandy!' breathed Emily Hope.

Irene Bailey looked over Mr Hope's shoulder. 'Oh! Poor things,' she murmured.

'They've had a terrible time,' Mandy informed them quickly. 'They're really sick, I think.'

'I'll go and get some supplies,' Mrs Hope said calmly, easing out of the bunker. Adam Hope knelt beside Melody, examining her carefully until Mrs Hope returned with a black leather bag. Harmony barked and dragged herself away as far as possible, into a corner. She lay with her head on her front flippers.

'What are you going to do, Dad?' Mandy urged. 'Can you help them?'

'We could take them down to the Research Station,' Irene Bailey suggested.

'Better not to move them just now,' Mr Hope suggested. 'I've got all the supplies I need to treat them right here.' He began looking inside the bag.

'They're called Harmony and Melody,' Mandy said quickly. 'We named them.'

Emily Hope uncoiled a long plastic tube from the vet's bag. 'They're definitely dehydrated. They're certainly very weak or they wouldn't take kindly to a bunch of strangers being so close.'

'That's what we thought,' Bart agreed.

'We'll start by easing this fishing net off the smaller seal. Then, we'll give them each a litre of water and glucose solution,' Adam Hope said.

'We tried feeding them,' Mandy reported. 'But they didn't seem interested.'

'They're too ill to want to eat,' Mrs Hope said.

'Are they going to be all right?' Mandy asked anxiously, as her father took a closer look at Harmony.

'There's no way of telling at this stage, love.' Mr Hope smiled at Mandy and Bart. 'But you've done really well, both of you.'

Emily Hope looked up, frowning. 'How on earth did you get the seals up here from the beach?' she asked. 'They must weigh a ton.'

'On Bart's sled.' Mandy smiled.

'Your quick thinking might have saved their lives,' said her mum warmly. She stood up and gave Mandy a hug. 'Now, let's get to work. We want to see these two back in the sea – as soon as possible.'

Six

It was nearing four o'clock, and the light was fading fast. Irene Bailey appeared with a bucket of warm water and a hurricane lamp. She struck a match and set it to the wick.

'Thanks, Irene,' said Emily Hope. She narrowed her eyes to examine the wounds made by the net on Melody's side. The seals flopped weakly; Melody's eyes were closed and Harmony blinked fearfully at the flickering flame in the lamp. Melody's breath rasped and her sides heaved.

Adam Hope shone the beam of his torch into the eyes of each seal in turn and took their temperatures. Then, while Emily Hope mixed the glucose solution, he spread a small towel over Melody's eyes, draping it over her head like a veil. The little seal was too weak even to shake it off.

'Mandy, you can help,' her father said. 'Put one leg on either side of her and tuck her flippers behind your ankles. And hold the towel in place, please.'

Mandy did as she was asked, stepping carefully and using her hands to tuck the pup's silky soft flippers behind her boots. Bart helped by passing cotton wool soaked in an antiseptic solution to clean the seal's injuries. As the injuries were washed, the net came free from where it had become embedded in the thick fur. Adam Hope gathered it up in his arms and threw it over the wall of the bunker.

'Thankfully, the wounds aren't too deep,' Emily Hope said, shifting from one knee to the other as she bathed the cuts. 'They're just skin wounds – but some are infected.'

Mandy could feel the seal breathing hard under her hands. She soothed the little pup with her fingers, stroking to try and offer her comfort.

Once Melody's cuts had been treated, Bart and

Mandy watched while Mr Hope inserted the long plastic tube into the mouth and stomach of each seal. A small funnel was fitted to the end of the tube and the mixture poured in it, very slowly. Harmony coughed and shook her head in protest at first, but Adam Hope made sure she took a whole litre. He did the same for Melody, who lay motionless from start to finish.

'There,' he said, straightening and handing Mandy the funnel. 'That will normalise their body fluids and make them feel a lot better.'

'We'll give them more in about four hours,' Emily Hope said.

'When might they want to eat, Mum?' Mandy asked.

'We'll try tomorrow,' said Emily Hope. 'If they're any stronger, we can add a little minced herring to the tube. We have to take it slowly.'

'OK,' Mandy nodded gravely. She reached out to Melody and touched her smooth head. The seal pup blinked at her. It seemed to Mandy as though her eyes were filled with gratitude.

Mandy thought how lucky she and Bart were to have come across the seal pups when they did. Bart was smoothing a hand over Harmony's sleek back. The bigger pup struggled to get out of the way, but only half-heartedly.

'You've been great, all of you,' said Irene Bailey, gathering up the bucket and tubes. 'I'll go and give these a wash out.'

'Thanks, Irene,' Emily Hope smiled. 'I could do with a cup of tea now!'

'I'm sure you could!' she laughed, as she went out of the bunker, adding, 'It's brewing in the kitchen.'

Mandy looked up at the sky studded with bright stars. She realised that she was numb with cold. The thought of a hot bath and something to eat was enticing, but she was reluctant to leave the seal pups.

As if sensing her concern, Emily Hope smiled at her. 'I'm sure they're going to be fine now,' she said softly. 'Let's leave them to settle. We can check on them again in a few hours.'

'OK,' Mandy nodded. 'I expect they'd like a bit of peace and quiet anyway.'

'Yes,' her father agreed. He carried the lamp to the door. Mrs Hope picked up the bag and Bart took the fish bucket. The seals watched them with their big, grave eyes.

Mandy was the last to leave the bunker. In her heart, she knew that they had done all that they could, but was it enough? Only time would tell whether the treatment the seals had received would be enough to help them regain their strength, in time to join a group of Harp seals travelling south.

After supper, Mandy and Bart were playing a board game in the sitting room when Adam Hope came in.

'Do you want to come and check on your two patients before bed?' he asked. Mandy and Bart jumped up eagerly. Mr Hope was already armed with a torch. Bart ran to light the hurricane lamp.

The seals were lying together against the far wall of the shed. The pups were still rather quiet and Adam Hope was able to lift their lips to check on the colour of their gums and look into their eyes with the torch.

'I think they're beginning to recover,' he said, sounding relieved. 'Let's see if they feel like eating a bit more.'

'OK.' Mandy smiled. She and Bart stroked the seals while her father inserted the long plastic tube

for the second time that day. This time, it was
Bart who straddled each seal, holding the funnel
steady while Mr Hope guided the tube, and
Mandy poured in the solution of water and
glucose.

It was freezing outdoors. There was ice forming
on the concrete floor of the bunker, which pleased
Mandy. That would make the enclosure feel more
like home to Melody and Harmony.

Bart yawned and stretched, gathering up the
tube and funnel and the empty bucket. 'I'm beat,'
he announced.

'Yes,' Adam Hope agreed. He pushed aside the
board covering the doorway. 'Let's all get some
rest now,' he said. 'It's been a long day – for all of
us.'

Mandy lay awake for a long time. She was glad that
Vivaldi, the cat, had chosen to sleep beside her for
a second night. He was warm and soft and, if
Mandy lay very still, she could feel a faint vibration
when the cat purred. She ran her fingers gently
across his silky coat, thinking about the seal pups.

She longed to see Melody and Harmony
completely well. She thought back to a holiday

she had spent with relatives on the Scottish island of Jura. She had helped to nurse Selkie, a sick baby seal, back to health. As much as Mandy had wanted Selkie to be well, it had been painful to say goodbye to the adorable little seal. Selkie had been set free into the safe waters of the bay, brimming with good health. Would Melody and Harmony be as lucky, she wondered?

On Sunday morning, Adam Hope prepared to give the seals more of the glucose solution via the stomach tube. This time, he added a little of the herring, minced up. 'I hope we'll see a big improvement today,' he said, as he opened the doorway to the bunker.

Bart and Mandy squeezed inside as unobtrusively as possible, and stood with their backs pressed to the wall. Melody and Harmony barked noisily and scrunched up together as soon as they came in. Mandy was pleased to see that Melody had lifted her head; her eyes looked a little brighter. Even better, big shining tears welled in her eyes again, and the skin around them was dark and moist. Mandy knew that was a sign that Melody was no longer dehydrated.

Adam Hope approached the pups cautiously, aware of the fact that they were gaining in strength and might attack out of fear. 'As they begin to feel better,' he said, speaking softly to Mandy and Bart, 'they will be more protective of this enclosed space they're in. They might get to be quite fierce,' he warned. 'We must be careful.'

'We will,' Mandy said solemnly. She watched as the seals' temperatures were taken, then it was her turn to gently sit astride them, holding the funnel in place while Bart poured in the mixture. The fish slithered down the tube; Harmony shook her head unhappily as Mr Hope held up her chin, stretching out her neck and throat to help the tube slip down. Melody, too, looked displeased at having a tube in her throat, but Mandy knew it was the only way to make sure they really got better.

When the feeding was over, Mandy, Bart and Adam Hope crouched down to watch the seals for a bit. Harmony rubbed her whiskery chin across the floor. She shook her head and smacked her lips, looking around her as if waking from a dream. Then she yawned and rolled over on to her side. She paddled her good flipper, and to

Mandy it looked as if the little seal was waving. Melody was less active. She slumped on her side, and sighed, as if she was worn out by the breakfast.

'We're going to have to get some more herring,' Adam Hope said. 'If they get well, they'll need about three kilograms a day.'

'Wow!' said Mandy.

'That's a lot!' Bart agreed.

Mandy couldn't help feeling worried about Melody, though. She still seemed so weak and the idea of her eating a whole kilo of fish three times a day seemed a long way off.

Steve Bailey telephoned a friend who was a fisherman. 'Good news,' he reported, when he'd hung up. 'My friend Jonas has a freezer full of herring. He's going to let us buy it for the seals.'

'It's just as well,' Mrs Bailey said. 'The food store in town is closed today.'

'Getting them both to eat without the tube is critical,' said Emily Hope. 'We can't think of releasing them until they show a real interest in food.'

'It's early days,' Adam Hope said. 'Let's get this fish, then we'll see.' Then he added, 'If you tell me where to go, I could take your truck, Steve?'

'It's not too far,' Mr Bailey said, reaching for a sheet of paper and a pen. 'I'll write down the directions for you.'

'Can I come, Dad?' Mandy asked.

'If you like.' Adam Hope reached for his coat and gloves. He tucked the folded paper into his pocket. 'Wrap up warm.'

'Are you coming, Bart?' Mandy shrugged on her thick jacket.

'I've got to finish a project for school tomorrow,' he answered. 'I'll see you later.'

'Drive carefully, Adam,' warned Emily Hope. 'Those roads are treacherous.'

'Don't worry, I will,' replied Mandy's dad.

'Bye, Mum,' Mandy called. She was very pleased they had managed to locate some more food for Melody and Harmony. She just hoped the pups would soon want to feed on their own, without the help of a tube.

'You can navigate,' Adam Hope said cheerfully, as they turned right out of the Baileys' driveway. He passed Mandy the directions and she smoothed them out on her knee. It was bitterly cold in the car and Mandy's breath clouded in front of her.

'Let's crank up the heating, Dad,' she smiled, fiddling with the knobs on the dashboard. The tyres crunched over the frozen snow along the road. In spite of the chains fitted to the wheels of the car, the going was slippery.

'Good idea,' said Mr Hope. Then, as the engine began to generate warmth, he added, 'That's better.'

Mandy looked out of the window. They had passed through the town of Nain and were heading out along the only tarred road, driving north. All around her the trees were stiff with frozen snow, their branches silhouetted against the white sky.

'Looks like more snow on the way,' Adam Hope remarked. He drove slowly, frowning with concentration. Mandy could see the white of his knuckles as he gripped the steering wheel. 'We're approaching a T-junction,' he announced. 'Which way now?'

'Left,' said Mandy. 'Towards the foothills of the Red Wine Mountains, it says here.'

The narrow road they had taken was closed in

by forest. Towering birch and spruce trees were frosted with clumps of snow, which looked impossibly heavy on the fragile branches. Mandy felt as if she and her father were alone in the world.

'We can't be far now from Jonas's . . .' Adam hope began, but his sentence was cut short.

'Dad! Look out!' Mandy screamed.

A caribou had appeared quite suddenly in the middle of the road. It had leapt from the forest and stood stiffly, transfixed by the glare of the headlights. Adam Hope jammed his foot hard on the brake.

But it was too late. Mandy heard the squeal of the tyres, then a resounding thud.

Adam Hope flung out an arm to protect Mandy as she was thrown forward against her seatbelt. The truck slewed sideways and spun around in the snow. It came to a stop amid a hissing and crunching of ice. Then there was silence.

Seven

'Are you hurt?' Adam Hope asked his daughter anxiously.

Mandy managed a small smile, even though her heart was bumping around with shock inside her chest. 'I'm OK,' she said. 'You?'

'Fine, just a bit shaken. That caribou came out of nowhere. I couldn't avoid it.' Mr Hope put on his gloves. He looked pale.

Mandy looked round. 'It's run off!' she gasped. 'Poor thing!'

'We'll have to go after it. It may be injured. Hurry, Mandy.' Adam Hope fumbled with his seat belt.

Mandy scrambled out of the car. She felt dizzy, her heart still hammering with the shock of the accident and her concern for the caribou. The eerie silence of the snowy forest pressed in on her. Mr Hope got out of the truck and went around the front to check for damage.

'There's no time for that now, Dad!' Mandy pleaded.

'It will help me to assess how hard the caribou has been struck,' he explained. Then he straightened up. 'That's not too bad. There's only a very shallow dent in the bumper.'

'Do you think the caribou *has* been hurt?' Mandy asked miserably. The lovely animal was nowhere to be seen. There was a line of cloven hoofprints in the snow, leading away into the forest. The sky had darkened with heavy cloud and the light was fading, making it hard to pick out the tracks the caribou had made.

Adam Hope shook his head. 'I'm not certain, Mandy, love.' He looked worried. 'It's lucky I wasn't going very fast.'

'Let's follow its tracks then,' Mandy urged. 'It might need help.'

'You're right,' her father agreed. He was already

rummaging in the back of the truck. 'I'll need a torch.' He tugged aside a large black tarpaulin. Underneath it was a first aid box with a red cross on its lid, a jack and a flashlight. 'I hope it has batteries in it,' he muttered. He switched it on, and the bright warmth of the light was cheering.

'Good old Steve,' Mr Hope said, relieved. 'Now, I'm going to have to move the truck on to the side of the road, Mandy. Then we'll take a look around.'

While her father moved the truck, Mandy hopped about from foot to foot, trying to keep warm. She wondered what the chances were of somebody passing by. They were on a remote road; dusk was falling. It didn't seem likely. She examined the snow, peering at the area around the animal's hoofprints. 'There's no blood, thank heavens,' she reported, when her father joined her.

'Good,' he said. He linked arms with Mandy and hurried her through a break in the trees, shining the torch on the prints in the snow. Pine needles were piled in drifts against the base of the trunks, giving off a strong, fresh smell. The dense, frozen forest seemed forbidding at first, but soon Mandy began to recognise unexpected signs of life. Crusty red and green lichens had painted the exposed parts of the trees, and tiny pale green ferns thrust their heads bravely through the carpet of snow on the ground.

Suddenly, a cluster of ice clinging to a branch fell with a thud, and Mandy jumped. She clung more tightly to her father's arm. The torchlight wavered as they stepped carefully, slowly, through the trees.

Adam Hope peered closely at the snow, looking for signs of the caribou's distinctive tracks. They picked them up, then lost them again.

'Listen!' Mr Hope whispered, stopping.

Mandy strained her ears. She heard a scuffling, shuffling sound, which lasted for a moment and then stopped again. 'Over there!' she pointed to where the sound had come from. 'I heard something!'

Her father cocked his head, listening intently. The sound came again, sounding oddly familiar but very bizarre in these surroundings. Mandy felt a thrill of surprise as she realised it sounded like the lowing of a cow.

'This way.' Her dad took charge, ducking

around a tree and walking carefully in the direction of the noise.

They came quite suddenly into a clearing. A small caribou was lying against the base of a tree trunk, its forelegs curled under it. It had the branch antlers Mandy recognised from Christmas cards. Thick greyish-brown fur covered its back, ending in a short white tail. Mandy gasped as the animal tried to struggle to its feet, and failed.

'Shhhh,' Mr Hope cautioned. 'Very quietly now.' He had crouched down and Mandy followed his example. They kept perfectly still, watching. She hardly dared to breathe, in case she frightened it even more. The young caribou's startled brown eyes were trained on them; it sniffed the air, nervously weighing up the threat the humans represented. Again, it tried to get up, but sank back down, breathing hard.

'I don't think he's going anywhere,' Adam Hope whispered. 'He seems to be stunned and maybe bruised, or a bone is broken somewhere. I hope not,' he added. Slowly, he got to his feet and turned, leading Mandy back the way they'd come.

'What are we going to do?' she whispered urgently.

'I don't want to take a chance and leave it,' her father explained. 'It'll have to be examined, and, if there is an injury, treated.'

Mandy nodded. Her face felt frozen. She tugged her woolly scarf up over the lower half of her face. Adam Hope fumbled in his coat pocket for his mobile phone as they walked back towards the road.

Mandy shone the torch on to the dialling pad of the telephone while her father punched in the Baileys' number. Standing close beside him, she heard with relief the sound of Irene Bailey's cheerful voice. 'Hello?'

Adam Hope quickly explained what had happened.

'Don't worry,' Mandy heard Mrs Bailey say. 'I'll get in touch with a friend who lives in that area. He runs the local Wildlife Rescue Centre. His name is Dale Rogers. He'll find you. There's only the one road going north.'

'Thanks, Irene,' Mr Hope said gratefully.

'Are you sure you're all right?' she asked, sounding concerned.

'Fine, just cold, and worried about the caribou,' he answered.

'Stay in the truck – keep warm,' she advised. 'Help is on the way!'

'Thanks. Bye.' Adam Hope switched off the phone.

'I heard what she said,' Mandy said. 'Someone's coming to help us.'

'That's right.' Her dad smiled. 'Someone who probably knows more about these woodland caribou than I do! What a relief.'

'Should we go back to it?' Mandy asked.

'No.' Mr Hope shook his head. 'We don't want to frighten it, and there isn't much we can do right now. We'd better just wait for Irene's friend.'

It seemed as if time had stood still to Mandy. The wait in their truck for the arrival of the man from the Wildlife Rescue Centre seemed endless. She and her dad played word games, but Mandy's thoughts kept drifting back to the caribou that was unable to stand – and to the two seal pups at home in urgent need of food. She was aching with cold and growing more concerned with each passing moment. At last, she gave a triumphant shout. 'Lights! Car lights!'

'Is this our man?' Adam Hope peered ahead, through the icy windscreen.

'Yes!' Mandy scrambled to get out. 'It's him . . . I can see the sign on the truck.'

The approaching vehicle, towing a trailer, slowed to a stop beside them. It had the logo for the Wildlife Rescue Centre painted on the side.

Mr Hope and Mandy hurried forward to introduce themselves to Dale Rogers, who had another man with him. Both men were tall and strong-looking, made even bigger by their huge hooded overcoats.

'Thanks for coming out,' Adam Hope said. 'I'm pretty sure the caribou has been injured. We tracked it down to just inside the forest, not far from the road.'

'Do you know how bad its injuries are?' Mr Rogers asked, frowning.

'Hard to tell, exactly,' Mandy's dad answered. 'I couldn't get very close to it, but it seems dazed and unable to stand.'

'Right. Well, thanks for taking the trouble to keep an eye on it, Mr Hope. Andy and I will follow you to it.'

Mr Rogers had a rolled-up canvas stretcher

under one arm and a bag slung over his shoulder. He had a powerful flashlight, too. He walked behind Mandy's father, and Mandy walked between Mr Rogers and the man called Andy.

The caribou was lying where they had left it. Its head was lolling but it looked up quickly as they approached, their boots crunching in the snow. Mandy saw the soft, shaggy dewlap on the underside of its long neck. When Dale Rogers turned the beam of his flashlight on to the caribou, it blinked and struggled to get up.

'Oh, poor thing,' Mandy whispered. She noticed that Andy was inching through the undergrowth, creeping up on the animal from the other side of the tree. While Dale Rogers kept the caribou's attention, Andy deftly wound a length of cloth around its head.

'Why's he doing that?' Mandy asked softly.

'They're better blindfolded, while we examine them,' Mr Rogers explained in a whisper. 'It helps to keep them calm.'

Andy managed to inject the caribou with a sedative, then swiftly he tied its front and back feet to stop it kicking out. Then, Mr Rogers and Adam Hope ran their hands along its long legs, feeling for a break and any sign of a wound.

'There's a fracture,' Dale Rogers said, when he reached the caribou's chest. 'It's a rib.'

Adam Hope nodded, confirming the diagnosis. His fingers pressed gently into the sides of the animal. The caribou lay quietly, flicking the ear that wasn't against the ground. The velvet soft, pale grey muzzle twitched as the caribou tried to identify the strange scent of the humans examining it. Mandy listened – the caribou was taking short, panting breaths. She ventured closer, and put out a hand to stroke it, hoping to soothe it. His beautiful, soft coat was charcoal grey with darker legs and muzzle.

'We'll take him to the centre,' Dale Rogers decided. 'He's going to need confining in a small space until that rib mends.'

Andy and Dale Rogers rolled out the canvas stretcher. It took all three men to lift the caribou on to the canvas and carry him back to the waiting trailer. Mandy directed the beam of the flashlight to light their way through the forest.

Soon the caribou was lying on a bed of straw in the trailer.

'He'll soon recover,' Dale Rogers told her. 'Don't

worry. Would you like to come and visit him at the centre?'

'Oh, yes, please,' said Mandy. 'I'd like that very much.'

'Right, we'll be off, then.' He turned to Adam Hope. 'Is your vehicle damaged?'

'No, it's fine, thanks. And, again, thanks for your help,' replied Mandy's dad.

'It's nice of you to have taken the trouble to stop,' Andy said, shaking Adam Hope's hand. 'Bye.'

'Bye,' Mandy said. Adam Hope turned to get into the truck, but Mandy stood for a moment, watching the caribou being driven away.

Arriving back at the Baileys' house, Mandy saw Mr Bailey fling open the front door. He peered out, then waved.

'We've been worried about you!' he called. 'Are you all right?'

'We're OK, thanks,' Adam Hope said. He followed Mandy up the steps and into the warm house. 'The caribou is in good hands, thankfully.'

'Mr Bailey,' Mandy began anxiously, pushing back her hood. 'Because we didn't make it to your friend's house, we didn't manage to get any food for the seals.'

'Ah, but I've managed to find some herring, Mandy!' He smiled at her. 'I went to see a fisherman I know. He let me have all that he had – not a lot, but it will do for a couple of days.'

Mandy felt relieved. 'Oh! Fantastic!' she breathed.

Emily Hope put her arms around her daughter. 'I'm glad you two are in one piece!'

'Oh, Mum! That poor caribou!' Mandy began to worry again.

'He shot out of the trees,' Adam Hope said. 'I tried to brake, but . . .' He shrugged.

'How badly injured is he, Adam?' Mrs Hope asked.

'He was certainly dazed, and we found a fractured rib, too,' he said. 'Dale Rogers has taken him in to the centre until he recovers.'

Irene Bailey took Adam Hope's dripping boots from him and propped them on the hearth beside the log fire. 'Dale is an expert,' she said. 'The animal is in very good hands.'

'I must go and see Melody and Harmony,' Mandy said, adding, 'Where's Bart?'

'He's visiting a friend,' his mother replied. 'He'll be back about seven.'

'Shall we go and feed the seals, then?' Mandy looked at her father and mother in turn, keen to see for herself any improvement in the health of the smaller pup.

Her father looked at his watch. 'Six o'clock,' he mused. 'This'll be their last feed today. I'll get our equipment.'

'I'll get the fish,' Steve Bailey offered.

'See you out there,' Mandy called, slipping out of the door.

Harmony barked and shied away from the flickering light of the lamp. Mandy set it down safely in a corner of the shed, and shut the door firmly behind her.

'Hello,' she said, speaking very softly. Melody raised her head and blinked at Mandy. Her nose worked, picking up Mandy's scent. She made a hissing noise, then lay down again and closed her eyes.

'Are you awake, Melody?' Mandy whispered. She moved a little nearer and peered at Melody. The seal pup still seemed very weak. She made no attempt to move away as Mandy approached. Her eyelids flickered. 'You've got to eat,' Mandy pleaded gently. 'You will get much stronger if you eat something. Bart and I want to put you back in the sea. But you'll never make it if you don't eat.'

The shed door creaked open, making Mandy jump. In the half-light, she looked up at Bart's puzzled face.

'Who're you talking to?' he asked.

'Just Melody,' Mandy said. 'She doesn't seem as perky as Harmony, Bart. I'm worried. She needs to eat on her own to survive.'

Bart crouched beside Mandy. 'I'm worried about her, too,' he said. In the silence, they listened to Melody's rasping breathing. Harmony squealed, then yawned. 'She looks a bit better,' Bart added brightly.

It was true. The bigger seal pup seemed much stronger and more energetic. She was using her flippers to propel herself around the floor. Reaching Melody's side, she nuzzled her with her nose, as though trying to rouse the pup. Melody made no response.

'How are they?' Emily Hope pulled the barricade to the bunker closed behind her. The lamp Mandy had brought cast sufficient light, so she switched off her torch and crouched down to look at the seals. Harmony barked.

'Hungry?' Mrs Hope asked her with a grin. She began to fix up the feeding tube. Bart sat astride Harmony, while Mandy's mum quickly inserted the tube. The seal seemed to know just what to expect, and this time she opened her mouth obligingly.

Mandy took several small pieces of minced herring and plopped them into the funnel, along with the glucose and water. She kept at it, until her mum held up a hand.

'That's enough,' she said. 'Let's keep some for Melody.'

When Mrs Hope began gently to withdraw the tube, Harmony clamped her sharp little teeth around its end and began to chew.

'Hey!' said Bart, surprised. 'Let go, Harmony.'

'That's an excellent sign,' said Emily Hope. 'She's doing really well. It means she's ready for some chunks of solid food.'

'Great!' Mandy said. She reached out and patted Harmony's warm flank.

But Melody had to be coaxed to lift her head

and open her small mouth. She hissed and writhed to escape the hands that held her, and shook her head weakly to try and dislodge the feeding tube. Mandy held tight to the funnel, and the water and glucose sloshed over the sides as the little seal resisted swallowing. She coughed up some of the fish.

In spite of her struggle, Emily Hope kept coaxing, until she felt that Melody had taken almost the required amount of liquid. She slipped the tube out and Melody shook her head and rolled over on to her side.

'Poor girl,' Mandy said softly. 'She really doesn't seem to want to eat.'

'She must,' Mrs Hope reminded her. 'Or she won't be able to go back to the wild.'

'Yes,' Mandy nodded, watching the seal closely. Melody's small head flopped again, and her eyes closed. Mandy's heart turned right over. Melody gave a great sigh. Next to her, Harmony squirmed and paddled about, getting as close as she could. Mandy felt that Harmony could sense that her companion was in distress, and she was offering comfort.

Gently, Mandy put out a hand. Her fingers

made contact with the smooth, silver-grey fur of Melody's curved back. She stroked the seal lovingly. 'Please get well,' she murmured. 'Please get well, so that you can sing in the sea again.'

Eight

'You're up early!' said Mrs Bailey, almost bumping into Mandy who was coming in through the front door.

'Dad and I have been out to see the seals,' Mandy said, pulling off her boots. 'Harmony's eating really well now.'

'And Melody?' Irene Bailey asked.

'She still has to have the water solution by tube,' Mandy admitted, as her father appeared in the hallway behind her.

'But we didn't have to mince the herring quite so small this time, love, did we?' Adam Hope said.

'And she took it down very well,' he added.

'That's true,' Mandy said, still wishing that Melody would show an interest in food, the way Harmony did. She followed Mrs Bailey through to the kitchen, shrugging off her coat as she went. 'She has to eat on her own,' Mandy said. 'She just *has* to.'

'And she will,' Mrs Bailey said reassuringly. 'Seals are hardy creatures, don't forget. I'm sure she won't starve herself to death.' She moved briskly around the kitchen, putting out things for breakfast.

'But she seems so weak.' Mandy frowned.

'She's still recovering,' Mrs Bailey smiled. 'She needs to conserve her strength.'

'Yes, I suppose so.' Mandy nodded. She smiled back at Mrs Bailey, adding, 'I'm going with Dad to the Wildlife Rescue Centre to see the caribou today.'

'I know – and Bart would have given anything to be able to go with you. I don't think his teacher would have been happy about that, though. He has a math test today!'

'Oh dear.' Mandy chuckled, then gave a thought to her own school assignments. She had neglected her schoolwork lately. She made a silent promise to herself to write her weekly letter to her class that evening, and to complete her science assignment, too.

'How are our two patients this morning?' Emily Hope came into the kitchen, looking at Mandy enquiringly. Her long, auburn hair hung loose around her shoulders, still wet from the shower.

'Melody took a bit of fish by tube,' Adam Hope reported, setting out the breakfast mugs that Mrs Bailey had handed him.

'Could I borrow your car, Irene?' Emily Hope asked. 'Then I could come back from the Research Station at lunchtime, and give her a feed.'

'Of course you can,' Mrs Bailey nodded.

'Oh, good.' Mandy was relieved. 'Thanks, Mum.' Melody and Harmony would be in expert hands while she and her dad visited the Wildlife Centre.

'What a wonderful smell!' Steve Bailey put his head around the door of the kitchen. Bart was behind him, his school bag over his shoulder.

'I'm baking some bread rolls,' Irene Bailey told him. 'Come and sit down. Emily, would you pour the coffee?'

* * *

Mandy navigated for a second time, while her father drove slowly along the ice-bound roads towards the Rescue Centre. In the main street of Nain, adults pulled small children and their shopping on sleds. Adam Hope drove out of the town, heading north on the only paved road there was. Around them lay the vast, trackless wilderness, covered in ice.

It wasn't a long drive and quite soon, Mr Hope turned the big vehicle into the driveway of the

centre. He came to a stop outside a clapboard outbuilding. Snow had iced the roof like a cake; icicles formed a lacework pattern as they clung to the gutters. Somewhere a dog barked, but Mandy couldn't see it. A tractor was parked beside a hillock of hay, covered by a sheet of black oilcloth.

Dale Rogers appeared at the door, wearing big survival boots and a hat with long earflaps. 'Hi there!' he called, beckoning them in. 'Come to see your caribou?'

'Has it recovered, Mr Rogers?' Mandy asked, stepping inside. The small room that served the centre as an office was crowded and haphazard. Electric heaters blasted warm air from noisy fans and a woman tapped at a computer keyboard. A telephone rang shrilly and she answered it in a low, friendly voice.

'He's still a bit sore, but apart from that he's doing fine,' Mr Rogers said. 'Do you want to see him?'

'Yes, please.' Mandy had to raise her voice to be heard.

'You couldn't have come at a busier time,' Mr Rogers commented, opening the door and stepping out into the cold. It was instantly quiet, except for the crunch of boots on the snow. 'We're trying to raise a bit of money for the centre, so we're planning an open day.'

'Good idea,' Mr Hope said, striding along beside Mr Rogers.

'When is it?' Mandy asked.

'The day after tomorrow – Wednesday,' he answered. 'It's the anniversary of our opening. We've got a wildlife expert coming in to give a talk on our resident animals, as well as a barbecue and hot apple cider . . .'

'Wow!' Mandy's eyes widened. 'What a great idea, bringing the community together for a great cause like injured wildlife!'

'I'm glad you think so! You must come along,' Mr Rogers said. 'It'll be lots of fun.'

'We'll certainly try and make it,' Mr Hope said. 'My wife and I are doing a research paper on the area and we've got to concentrate on meeting our deadlines!'

'I sympathise.' Dale Rogers smiled, as he led them to a series of fenced pens.

In the first pen, lying with his long legs folded under him on a heap of straw, was the caribou that had collided with the front of Steve Bailey's truck. 'Here's the young fella.' Mr Rogers pointed. 'We've put him in a smaller pen than usual so he doesn't move around too much, which gives that rib a chance to heal.'

'Oh,' breathed Mandy. For the first time, in the clear light of morning, she was able to see the animal close at hand. He was even more beautiful! His large, caramel-coloured eyes regarded her gravely. The thick fur was flecked with white, but it was the complex pattern of his heavy antlers that particularly interested Mandy. The caribou got stiffly to his feet, and backed as far away as his small enclosure would allow.

Dale Rogers began to blow softly through nearly closed lips, trying to calm the nervous creature. 'Many of the animals that end up here have never seen human beings before,' he explained. 'If they're lucky, they may never see one again, once we release them back into the wild.'

The caribou lowered his head and shook his antlers from side to side.

'Why was this caribou alone, Mr Rogers?' Mandy was curious. 'I thought they were always in a herd.'

'Mostly, they are,' Mr Rogers agreed. 'But there

are also small family groups and lone animals. They live in herds for much of the year, migrating south to their wintering grounds in fall. They only stop for the rut – when the males fight one another for the attention of the females.'

The caribou wagged its stumpy white tail, flicking it back and forth. Mandy saw that the tip of one antler had broken off. It was a young male; perhaps it had been fighting. The caribou turned his back, dipping his head gracefully to lick at his foreleg.

'When do you think he'll be completely well again?' Mandy asked.

'After about ten days,' Dale Rogers replied. 'As soon as that bone has knitted, he can go.'

The caribou looked up, tensing his ears, as though he had understood. Mandy imagined him streaking away to freedom across the snowy tundra.

'Where will you release him?' Adam Hope asked.

'Pretty much in the area where we collected him,' Mr Rogers said. 'There might be other members of a herd still in the vicinity.'

'That's a nice thought,' Mandy smiled. 'Thanks for rescuing him, Mr Rogers.'

'I'm glad I could help.' He grinned at her. 'Now, would you like to take a look around? Do feel free to have a wander.'

'You've been great,' Mr Hope said. 'Thanks so much.'

Mandy and her father wandered around, meeting Dale Rogers' staff of volunteers and his hard-working wife Michelle, who had once been a veterinary nurse in Quebec. Mandy and her father came across her hand-feeding a white Arctic fox.

Mandy pressed her forehead to the wire of the pen. She was enchanted. 'Ah,' she said softly. 'How lovely!'

'Hello, I'm Michelle Rogers,' said Michelle, looking up. 'You're the people who had the collision with the caribou?'

'That's right.' Mandy nodded.

'We're really glad Irene called us,' Michelle told them. 'Too often animals get left behind after an accident like yours.'

'It was no problem,' said Mr Hope.

When Mrs Rogers returned to her task, they moved on. Mandy saw several huge logs being dragged into a towering pile and wandered over to investigate. 'What's this for?' she asked a man who was busy stacking smaller logs on to the pile.

'To keep our visitors warm on Open Day!' he answered, smiling at her. Nearby, someone was setting out a row of litter bins. On them had been painted in bright red letters: *Don't litter, please*! The germ of an idea began to form in Mandy's mind.

When the cold had finally driven them back to the shelter of the centre's little office, Mandy and Mr Hope told Dale Rogers all about their own rescued animals.

'Ah, yes!' he said enthusiastically. 'Irene Bailey told me about the seal pups. Good for you!'

'The beach is a disgrace,' Michelle Rogers added, joining them. 'There are loads of rusting tin cans and bottles left by the fisherman.'

'And nets . . . and hooks,' Mandy put in. 'It needs a clean-up. My friend Bart thinks so too. He lives right above the beach.'

'It's a problem,' Mr Rogers agreed, shaking his head, 'that's for sure.'

'Well, we'd better start back,' Adam Hope said. 'I don't plan to do any driving in the dark after my last experience. Thanks again, Dale.'

'Yes, thanks, Mr Rogers,' Mandy smiled.

'It was great to meet you both,' said Mr Rogers. 'Don't worry about the caribou. We'll take good care of him.'

Mandy waved as she climbed into the truck. She felt very relieved to know that the caribou was getting better and would soon be free.

In the meantime, there were Melody and Harmony to think about, as well as the idea that was steadily taking shape in Mandy's mind. 'Dad! I've had an amazing idea!' she began excitedly, turning to him as he eased the truck out of the gates of the centre. 'You know the Open Day the Wildlife Centre is holding? Well, if Mr and Mrs Bailey agree, we could organise our own event to get people in the town involved in cleaning up the beach.'

'Sounds good,' Mr Hope said, raising his eyebrows.

'We could invite everyone to a beach barbecue,' Mandy went on, finding herself filling with energy. 'Bart and I could design some posters and put them up around the town and at the Research Station . . . maybe even at Bart's school. We could invite everyone to help pick up the litter and in return, we'll give them some delicious food . . .'

'It's a really great idea, love,' Adam Hope agreed. 'But it'll take some organising.'

'I could do that,' Mandy assured him. 'We could make a huge fire on the beach, like Mr Rogers is doing for his Open Day. Everyone could huddle around it and drink warm cider and eat hot dogs and . . .'

'Well, I think you might have something there,' Mandy's dad grinned at her. 'It's certainly a good cause.'

'It's a brilliant cause!' Mandy insisted. 'I can't wait to get home to tell Bart all about it.'

She settled back in her seat to plan some more. There was going to be a lot to do, in between taking care of Melody and Harmony. Thinking of the smaller seal made Mandy's stomach lurch. If they got back soon, she would be in time to see her mum do the next feed. Mandy willed the miles to pass quickly so she could see how the little seal was getting on.

When they reached the Baileys' house, Mandy went straight to the bunker. Bart was already there, sitting cross-legged on the floor, gazing at Melody. The wooden barricade had been pulled open and

Harmony had ventured out into the yard. Mandy didn't spot her at first, but Bart pointed the seal out. Harmony was sleeping in an uncomfortable looking position, with her flipper sticking into the air. Her smooth black nose was buried in the snow.

'My mom said to let her out,' Bart explained, when Mandy looked surprised to see Harmony out of the bunker. 'Seals hate being in a confined space.'

'Oh, OK,' Mandy said. 'How's Melody?' She stooped to look at the little seal.

'She been grooming herself,' Bart reported. 'That's a good sign. Your mum's on the way over with the tube for her next feed.'

Mandy settled on her haunches. The seal gazed at her with solemn black eyes. Chunks of herring lay here and there on the floor, but Melody still didn't seem the least bit interested. Mandy reached into the bucket and took up a handful of the fish. She rolled it around in her fingers, making it into a firm little ball. Then she tossed it lightly across to Melody. It landed with a splat beneath her nose. Melody sniffed at it. Then, to Mandy's delight, she opened her mouth and snatched it up, swallowing it down with a loud gulp.

Mandy gasped. 'Bart! That's great!'

'Wow,' he breathed. 'She actually did it. She ate something!'

'Success?' Emily Hope enquired, looking round the opening of the bunker. In her hand she held the bucket and feeding tube.

Mandy jumped up. 'Mum! She's just this minute eaten a mouthful of herring!'

'What a relief.' Mrs Hope smiled. 'That's really good news. It means she's on the mend.' She put down the bucket and watched as Melody scooted across the floor, sniffing. She found another piece of fish, and ate that too.

'Oh, good girl,' Mandy sighed, feeling hugely thankful. Melody smacked her lips, and twitched her whiskers, making little slapping noises on the floor with her tail.

'She wants more,' announced Bart, tossing her more of the fish. In a trice, the pup swooped on it and swallowed it whole. Mandy and Bart cheered and gave her more fish. Eventually Mrs Hope suggested that Melody had had enough.

'She's better,' Mandy beamed. 'She's really feeling better.' Her eyes were shining. 'Let's go and tell the others the good news.'

Nine

Adam Hope and Mr Bailey were delighted to hear the news that Melody had started to feed on her own. Mr Hope went out to take the temperature of both seals and, when he came back inside, he looked very pleased. 'What an improvement!' he said, patting first Mandy, then Bart, on the back. Then he looked serious. 'Now that the seals are feeding, they'll be able to generate heat inside their bodies. Because of their thick layer of blubber and because seals don't sweat, it is sometimes difficult for them to get cool, if they're not in the water – and they can become dangerously hot. We'll have to keep an eye on that.'

'Right.' Mandy nodded. 'How could we cool them down?'

'A hosepipe should do it,' Steve Bailey suggested.

'Great.' Bart grinned.

'As they become stronger, they'll be less docile, too,' Emily Hope warned. 'It'll be best not to get too close to them now, just in case they decide to nip.'

'OK,' Mandy agreed. She would have to resist stroking Melody and Harmony, and keep her distance from them, but it would be worth it to see them restored to good health.

Mandy was longing to tell the Baileys and her mum about her idea for a beach barbecue. But she had to wait until supper was ready, and they were all sitting down in one place. 'Visiting Dale Rogers' place has given me an idea,' she began. 'He's having an Open Day, with a barbecue and things like that. I thought we could use the same idea to invite people to the beach, to help us clean it up. We could make a huge fire, and cook some food . . .'

'Brilliant!' Bart exclaimed, his mouth full.

'It might work.' Irene Bailey looked thoughtful.

'I know a lot of people who are concerned about the mess down there.'

'If the people in Nain all agree something needs doing about the beach, that's an excellent start,' Emily Hope said.

'When will we do it?' Bart asked.

'How about Sunday?' suggested Irene Bailey. 'That would give us enough time to get ready.'

'So . . . we can do it?' Mandy asked. 'You agree?'

'Sure.' Steve Bailey nodded. 'I'm game.'

'We'll need to work out the details,' ventured Mrs Bailey, smiling at Mandy's enthusiasm. 'Food, and such . . .'

'Of course!' Mandy cried. 'We will. We'll do it now, if that's OK?'

'Finish eating,' her mum advised.

Mandy sprang up the moment she swallowed her last mouthful, and left the table to fetch a pen and some paper. She and Bart began by making a list of the Baileys' friends and colleagues.

'That's twenty-two people, counting the six of us,' Bart said. 'We could design a poster, and put it up at the Research Station – and my school, too.'

'Yes,' Mandy agreed. 'We'll have to make it look really fun, so people will want to come and help.

After all, it isn't a very big beach – just a dirty one.'

'People will need a real incentive for coming,' Steve Bailey pointed out, peering over Mandy's shoulder at the list. 'It's very cold, and it'll be strenuous work combing that beach.'

'Hot dogs!' Bart put in. 'That'll get them to come.'

'Yes!' Mandy laughed excitedly. 'And hot chocolate, jacket potatoes, and roasted marshmallows!'

Bart nodded. 'Yes, that's the sort of thing.'

'We can invite everyone who volunteers their time to a dessert and warm apple cider back here – that is, if they've got the energy to get back up the hill!' Mrs Bailey offered.

'Thanks, Mrs Bailey!' Mandy said, delighted. 'That would be great.' She looked at each of the adults in turn. She knew that her parents worked late into the night, sitting quietly at the small desk in Steve Bailey's study. 'I know how busy all of you are, but it'd be so nice if you could help.'

'Of course we'll help,' her dad said cheerfully. 'It's for a very good cause.'

'I agree,' Mrs Hope said. 'In the short time we've

been here, we've already seen how much damage the litter on the beach causes.'

'Mr Ross,' Bart said suddenly, remembering the old man who had found the injured snow goose. 'He'll definitely help.'

'And Maria, at work . . . and your dad's friend at the gas station . . . what's his name?' Irene Bailey frowned.

'Pierre!' Bart exclaimed. He scribbled the name on the list.

By the end of the afternoon, they had compiled their list and completed most of the telephoning, too. Bart and Mandy sent out invitations to those people whose e-mail addresses were known, and then settled down to design some posters. Steve Bailey began flipping through a recipe book that had belonged to his grandmother.

'What are you looking for?' his wife asked him.

'I thought I'd make my special chocolate fudge brownies, for afters,' he said.

'Now that will definitely make me pick up rubbish for an afternoon!' joked Adam Hope.

On Tuesday morning, the seal pups seemed brighter. They had grown used to the comings and goings of Mandy, Bart, and Emily and Adam Hope, and greeted their visitors with a chorus of noisy barking. Melody had joined her companion in the yard, and both seals seemed reluctant to venture back into the enclosed bunker.

Mandy kept her distance, throwing chunks of fish to them when feeding time came round. Though Melody's fur was still scarred by the cuts made by the fishing net, the wounds had healed and her small, rounded body was growing even plumper. She looked longingly at Mandy, and often tried to approach her. She waddled along through the snow, her nose twitching eagerly, but Mandy stayed well back.

'Seals are sociable creatures,' Adam Hope had warned her. 'That's why they're easily trained. We must take care that they don't get too attached to us.'

Mandy thought about what her father had said and backed away from an eager Harmony, who had slithered up on her other side. The bold pup had shuffled closer to her hand than she had dared to before. The seals were almost ready to be released, and they had to be kept as wild as possible, to ensure their safe and successful return to the ocean. Although the thought of seeing them go saddened Mandy, she knew it was what they needed most of all.

The snow held off all morning, and Harmony's temperature began to rise. She was overheating in her thick, blubbery coat, and Adam Hope expressed concern.

'We should cool them down with a hose,' he suggested.

Emily Hope looked at her watch. 'We'll be late for our appointment at the Research Station,' she said.

'And I'll be late for school!' Bart grinned.

'But we have to do it!' Mandy said. 'Come on . . . Dad? Mum?'

'All right,' Emily Hope decided.

Bart uncoiled a long green hosepipe from the basement of the house. He connected it to a second hosepipe and attached it to the tap in the laundry room. It snaked up through the middle of the house and ran down the steps to the front door, just reaching the yard.

'Fantastic,' Mandy said enthusiastically.

Bart only half-opened the tap, so that the spray of water was not too fierce. The seals eyed Mandy

warily; they seemed to sense something was going on.

'They might not like it,' Emily Hope cautioned.

But Harmony loved it! The moment she felt the cold spray of water on her back she rolled over, rubbing her forehead on the floor and grunting softly with pleasure. Melody was more timid at first. She opened her mouth and shook her head, sending droplets flying in all directions. Bart and Mandy took turns spraying, laughing at the joyful expressions on the seals' faces.

'We might as well give the floor of the bunker a good wash while we're at it,' Mandy said.

'How are they liking it?' Emily Hope and Irene Bailey had come to watch the seals being sprayed.

'Having a great time,' chuckled Bart, peering over Mandy's shoulder.

When the coats of the pups and the bunker floor were gleaming, Bart ran to turn off the tap.

Harmony seemed disappointed by the end of the water. She looked around her, then rolled over on to her back and flapped her flippers, as though impatient for the water to start again. Melody was intrigued by the hosepipe, snaking away across the snow as Bart tugged it into a coil. She hurried after it and watched with a puzzled look as it disappeared into the basement window.

Mandy realised that the seals were getting far too energetic to be confined in the yard for much longer. They would have to be returned to the sea – and soon.

As though she had read Mandy's mind, Emily Hope suddenly spoke. 'It's time for them to go,' she said quietly. She turned and looked at Mandy. 'They're well enough. Do you agree, love?'

Mandy's heart gave a little jump. She didn't want to see them leave, but she knew her mother was right. 'Yes, Mum,' she said. 'When?'

'How about Saturday?' Mrs Hope looked at Irene Bailey.

'Sounds fine,' she said. 'Then Steve and Adam will be around to help us. It's time.'

Mandy was pleased at the response that their invitation to a 'clean-up' provoked. Bart had tacked up their poster in the foyer of his school on Tuesday morning, and by that evening, the telephone at the Baileys' house began to ring. Mr and Mrs Bailey, Bart and Mandy took turns answering, and wrote down any offers of donated food or driftwood for the big fire they were planning. Mandy's parents had not yet returned from the Research Station, where they were conducting a late interview with a local scientist.

Mrs Bailey was on the telephone when the doorbell rang. Mandy opened the front door to a local fisherman.

'Hello,' she said.

The man thrust a parcel wrapped in newspaper towards her. 'I've heard about your seals,' he explained. 'I have a little extra herring. Could you use it for them?'

'That's very kind!' Mandy smiled. 'Yes, we need all the fish we can get. Thank you.' She accepted the ice-cold packet, and then invited the man to the beach barbecue on Saturday.

'I'll bring my wife, and my children,' he promised, putting out his hand for Mandy to shake. She shook his woolly mitten. 'Arthur Shultz,' he said.

'I'm Mandy Hope,' she replied solemnly. 'See you on Saturday – and thanks again for the herring.' She closed the door and hurried into the kitchen to add the fish to the supply for the seals in Irene Bailey's freezer.

* * *

'We haven't had a single refusal!' Bart exclaimed. 'It's going to be great.'

They were on their way to the Open Day at the Wildlife Rescue Centre. Bart and Mandy were sitting side by side in the back of Mr Bailey's four-by-four while Emily Hope drove.

Mr Hope had the map open on his knee. 'There it is, Emily.' He pointed. 'Up ahead on the left.'

Mandy saw the familiar gates and turned to her friend. 'I'm so glad you were able to come with us today, Bart,' she said.

'Wednesday is the best day of the school week for me – early closing,' he grinned.

Mrs Hope turned into the driveway. Mandy was surprised to see the number of vehicles parked in an orderly row outside the office. 'There's been a good turn-out,' she said. 'That's great.'

They joined a group of visitors who were gathered in a barn. Children sat on the floor, their mouths open, gazing up at a man who was giving a talk. On his shoulder sat a large white owl with yellow eyes.

'It's a snowy owl!' Emily Hope whispered, as they edged into the crowd. Mandy listened in delight as the man told fascinating stories about the owls and eagles that lived in this amazing climate.

When the talk was over, people strolled around the centre, sipping hot cider from paper cups and admiring the recovering animals. The caribou had drawn a lot of interest. He stood at the edge of his enclosure, looking bright-eyed and curious, and Mandy saw that he was walking much more easily.

'He's a beauty!' Emily Hope said. 'Look at those antlers.'

Michelle Rogers was packing hot dog sausages into bread rolls while her husband was allowing the children to pet the Arctic fox Mandy had met on her previous visit. There were donation tins everywhere and Mandy was pleased to see people dropping in lots of coins.

'How are the seal pups?' Dale Rogers asked, when the crowd he had attracted had drifted away.

'Really well.' Mandy grinned. 'The smaller one is eating on her own at last.'

'And how are your plans for tackling that beach coming along?' he asked her.

Mandy fished into the pocket of her jacket. 'Here,' she said, pulling out an invitation. 'This is for you and your wife. Will you come?'

'Sounds like a good idea,' he smiled. 'We'll be there, Mandy.'

'Thanks, Mr Rogers,' she said. 'It's going to be a lot of fun.'

Mandy's dad was admiring the big, portable gas barbecue the Rogers were using. 'Any chance of my borrowing this for our beach party on Saturday, Dale?' he asked. 'It looks very efficient.'

'Sure, no problem,' he replied. 'I'll give it a clean-up and bring it over to you on Saturday morning.'

'Thanks, Mr Rogers.' Mandy grinned. She knew her dad wanted to head for home before dusk set in, but she wanted to say a final goodbye to the caribou.

'Give me a minute, please, Dad,' she pleaded. The beautiful animal looked over the fence at her, chewing slowly on some hay. Gently, Mandy pushed her fingers into the soft, thick fur of his back and silently wished him well on his journey to find his family. The caribou raised his head and gazed at Mandy with deep, dark brown eyes.

'Good luck,' she whispered. 'Take care of yourself, now.'

'Saying goodbye?'

Mandy jumped. Dale Rogers was standing beside her.

'Yes, I was,' she admitted.

'He's going to be fine,' Mr Rogers assured her. 'I reckon we'll release him within the next couple of days. You did him a good turn. He might have died otherwise.'

'I'm glad he's better.' Mandy beamed. 'And I'm glad he's going home.'

'Are you coming?' called Emily Hope from the truck. 'I'm freezing!'

'Just coming!' Mandy called back. 'Bye, Mr Rogers.' As she ran to join her parents, Mandy's thoughts were with Melody and Harmony. Soon, her beloved little seals would face a journey back to freedom, too.

Mandy woke early on Saturday morning. She lay in bed, her hand resting on Vivaldi's back, thinking about Melody and Harmony. Today would be a test of their recovery. The day before, Mandy had noticed that the ice lay thickly along the shore now, leaving no visible channels of water in which the seals could swim out to the deeper ocean. There had been no sighting, either, of a

passing group of Harp seals to look after the pups
on their journey south. Mr Bailey had explained
that there was no way of being certain whether a
group would even accept Harmony and little
Melody. Mandy's heart tightened as she thought
of all the obstacles they still faced. But it was the
only way forward. It had to work.

Mandy got up, too worried to lie still a moment
longer. The cat grumbled his disapproval. She
slipped on her warm dressing gown and slippers
and went into the sitting room. Steve Bailey was there
already, looking out of the picture window. As she
came in, he lifted a pair of binoculars to his eyes.

'Any seals passing, Mr Bailey?' Mandy asked
quietly.

'*Look*, Mandy,' he said. 'A fantastic sight.' He
handed her the glasses. 'It's a whole group,
heading south.'

'Oh! Thank goodness!' Mandy put the binoculars
to her eyes. Out on the frozen wilderness, several
hundred plump, dark shapes had come into focus.
She gasped. 'There are so many of them!' To Mandy
they looked like flakes of chocolate on a huge
vanilla ice cream. The seals were a dream come
true!

'Mum! Dad!' she shouted, not caring that it was still early.

'Yes, wake them. Wake everyone up. We should take Melody and Harmony down to the shore right away,' Mr Bailey said excitedly. He pointed out of the window. 'The Harp seals are on the move, and our pups need to join them – and soon.'

'Yes!' Mandy cried happily. It was just what she had hoped for – a chance for the two pups to have a group to travel with.

'I'll go and wake Irene and Bart,' Mr Bailey said. 'Get dressed – hurry, or . . .'

But Mandy was out of the room before he finished the sentence.

Steve Bailey had lined the back of his open truck with a canvas sheet. He was rinsing it off hastily with a bucket of water when Emily and Adam Hope came stumbling out of the front door. Zipping up her jacket as she appeared at the door, Mrs Bailey had a flask tucked under her arm.

'This is excellent luck, Steve,' said Adam Hope, tying his bootlace.

'Brilliant,' Emily Hope agreed. She hastily tucked

her long hair into the rim of her woollen cap.

'This may be one of the last migrating groups,' Irene Bailey told them. 'It's getting late in the season, so we must grab our chance to introduce Melody and Harmony to them.'

'We'll need something strong to lift them on.' Mr Bailey looked thoughtful. 'Any old blanket will do. Bart?'

Mandy turned to Bart, who looked asleep on his feet. His breath formed like smoke in the icy air. 'Quick!' she prompted him.

Bart hurried off to the house to find something suitable. He was back in an instant, with a couple of blankets in his arms.

Taking them from him, Adam Hope led the way to the seals. Harmony was lying on her back in the yard, her pale tummy exposed to the air. Melody was using her flippers to play with the snow, pushing it into small ridges, then nosing it around. She sneezed as they approached. Harmony gave a welcoming bark, obviously expecting her breakfast.

Bart had brought a bucket of fish. He waited while Mr Bailey and Adam Hope spread one of the blankets out on the ground.

'Right,' said Mrs Hope. 'Toss a bit of fish on to

the middle of the blanket – my bet is that Harmony will go for it first.'

Mandy reached into the bucket and groped around until she had an icy fish tail in her gloved hand. She threw it lightly on to the blanket, where it landed dead centre.

'Good shot,' Bart observed.

Harmony flopped across towards this unexpected treat, barking in delight. The moment she was on the blanket, Adam Hope and Mr Bailey sprang forward to wrap and lift her. They carried her, swinging, across to the truck.

'Ooh!' Mr Hope groaned. 'She's a load.'

Melody was next. She, too, waddled curiously on to the second blanket seeking a treat and was swiftly wrapped up and lugged outside. It took all four adults to heave the seals across to the far end of the truck, where they lay, squirming nervously under their woolly covering.

'Oh, poor things!' Mandy said sympathetically.

'It's a short journey,' Emily Hope soothed. 'They'll soon be back on the beach.'

Emily Hope and Mrs Bailey volunteered to walk down to the shore, while Mandy and Bart rode in the back of the truck with the seals. Mr Bailey drove, and Mandy's dad sat beside him.

It was a very different journey to the one they'd made to the house with the seals on the sled. Now, as the truck snaked its way down the steep hill to the beach below, the blankets rose and fell as Melody and Harmony tried vigorously to escape.

'Hang on tight,' Bart warned Mandy, as Mr Bailey swerved round a corner. Melody popped her head out. The seal blinked and shook her head, looking around her in a bewildered fashion. Bart hurriedly covered her over and held her tight. Mr Hope, looking out through the back window, gave him the thumbs-up sign.

'Hurry, Mr Bailey,' Mandy shouted. 'They're really restless.'

The truck lurched and bumped across the stony beach and came to a stop just a metre from the shore. As Bart's father cut the engines, it was strangely silent, with not even the familiar sounds of the waves washing on to the beach. The encroaching ice was much closer now than it had been just a few days before. There was just a thin strip of pale grey water between the beach and the pack ice. In the clear, cold light of the early morning, Mandy peered out across to the frozen horizon, looking for the group of seals. It seemed a hostile and barren place and her heart turned over, thinking of Melody and Harmony making their way out there – alone – to a new life.

Suddenly, she saw an inky black head burst from the channel and head for the ice. Others followed, and soon the ice was littered with plump, dark bodies. In the still, crystal air, the sound of barking floated across to the shore.

'Thank goodness,' Mandy said, who had been silently dreading that the seals would have gone before they made it down to the beach.

'Loads of them!' cried Bart. He leaped down from the truck, and clicked open the locks to the back flap. Mr Bailey and Adam Hope stood ready to lift the seals on to the shore.

'Yes, it is a big group.' Steve Bailey had put his binoculars to his eyes. He turned as his wife and Emily Hope joined them, both slightly out of breath from the climb down the hill.

'Ready?' Mrs Hope smiled, looking at Mandy.

'Ready,' she said, straightening her shoulders determinedly.

Mr and Mrs Hope, with Bart and his father, seized the blankets and swung the seals out in their hammocks, lowering them gently on to the stony beach. Mandy's heart thumped hard as she watched Mr Bailey carefully uncover them, unwrapping them like a precious parcel.

Four large dark eyes looked grave and wary. Melody's nose went up and she breathed in deeply. The scent of the sea, the salt and the thick ice was all around. Harmony barked and pushed herself forward off the blanket. She examined the stones, sniffing and looking around her. Then she looked over at Melody and made a small whimpering noise.

'Go . . .' Mandy said, to herself. 'Go now . . . quickly, please.' She held her breath as Melody launched herself off the blanket. She shuffled across to be close to Harmony. Pressed together, side by side, they began to propel themselves rapidly towards the big chunk of smooth ice sitting solidly just off shore.

'Oh!' breathed Mandy. Her hands flew to her mouth. 'They're really leaving, Bart.'

'Go for it!' Bart murmured. 'Good luck.'

Harmony was in the lead, pushing ahead

strongly. She reached the water, paddled her flippers, and Mandy cheered inwardly as she saw the freezing water break and ripple over Harmony's sleek back. The seal hauled herself out on to the ice chunk and from there, she lifted her head to study the scattering of sleek, dark bodies basking on the floe further out to sea. She sniffed the air, as if trying to identify them. Melody pushed after her, clambering up on to the thick shelf of jutting ice. She, too, gazed out at the seals huddling together.

'Bye!' Mandy called softly, hoping Harmony and Melody would turn so she could see their beloved faces just one more time.

And then, Melody did turn. She looked directly at Mandy and scooted around on her back flipper. She raised her head and gave a joyous bark. Then she began to waddle back to the shore, straight towards Mandy, as fast as her flippers would go.

Ten

'No!' Mandy cried, as the little seal dived sleekly into the water and swam towards her. 'Go back!'

Mandy waved her arms, but Melody kept on coming. Harmony, too, was turning about, making her way back to the people she knew.

'Right,' said Adam Hope, folding his arms and frowning. 'This might be tricky . . .'

'We tried not to tame them, or anything,' Mandy began, looking at each of her parents in turn.

Mrs Hope put an arm around her shoulders. 'We know that,' she said gently. 'I don't think they have become tamed really. It's just that they are not quite sure where their next meal is coming from!'

'They don't know what to do!' Bart pointed out.

'If only the seals on the ice were a little bit closer,' said his mother.

'Yes,' Mr Bailey agreed. 'You're right, Bart. I don't think these two pups know quite what is expected of them.'

'Can't we take them out there?' Mandy pointed, looking at Mr Bailey. 'Out to the pack ice, I mean?'

'No, Mandy.' He shook his head. 'I couldn't allow that. At this time of the year, the ice isn't completely hard in places. It might be dangerous.'

'Oh,' she said. On the beach, Melody and Harmony were greeting each other like long lost friends, having been separated for the first time in a week by a distance of a few metres. They rubbed noses and made little wheezing noises, and Mandy felt a fierce affection for them. She longed to welcome them back with a stroke and a tasty treat, but she knew she couldn't. She was torn, happy they'd come back, yet worried for them.

Adam Hope, with Irene Bailey, tried shooing the pups back out to the ice. Harmony cocked her head, gazing quizzically at them. Melody rolled over on to her side, and flapped her flipper. She yawned and stretched. She seemed content to breathe in the sea air and feel the stony pebbles under her back. Emily Hope clapped her hands sharply, hoping to scare them into taking off, but none of their tactics were any use. The seals stayed where they were.

The bitter cold was beginning to seep into Mandy's bones. Her mum's lips were turning blue. Mandy watched sadly as the last of the migrating Harp seals vanished under the water. Melody and Harmony had missed their chance.

They stood in silence for a minute.

'We'd better take them back,' Mrs Bailey suggested finally, handing Mrs Hope a steaming cup from her flask.

'We'll try again, maybe tomorrow,' said Mr Bailey heavily. He spread out the two blankets and dropped a bit of fish into each. Obediently, Melody and Harmony went after their treats, lolloping like clumsy puppies. Adam Hope pounced, wrapping them up. They were carried to the back of the truck once more.

*   *   *

Sunday was a clear, bright day, the perfect day for the beach clean-up – and there was a lot to do, even without the worry of setting the seals free. Early in the morning, Mandy took up her vigil at the picture window, scanning the sea and the ice for signs of seals. But there were no dark rounded heads to be seen.

'There aren't any out there today,' she said, turning as her mother came in.

'Seals?' Mrs Hope raised her eyebrows.

Mandy nodded sadly.

'There'll be more coming along the coast, heading south,' Mandy's mum said reassuringly. 'I'm certain of it.' But Mandy could tell that her mother wasn't really all that certain.

Mandy shrugged. 'I hope so.' There was nothing for it but to wait patiently until the next passing group of seals appeared out on the pack ice.

Mrs Bailey popped her head round the door. 'Morning!' she called. 'Busy day, today! Mandy, could you give me a hand in the kitchen? Bart's just gone out to feed the seals.'

Mandy nodded and put away the binoculars. At least today she wouldn't have time to sit around worrying about the seals.

'Ketchup, buns . . . paper napkins.' Irene Bailey was loading things into a basket to be ferried out to the truck.

'Enough for an army!' Mandy smiled.

'It's a good thing that I buy food in bulk during the summer and autumn,' she replied. 'There wouldn't be enough to buy in the stores at this time of year!'

When the truck was loaded up, Mandy and Bart went to bundle up in their warmest clothing. It took time, squeezing on layer after layer, and Mandy felt she looked a bit like Santa Claus at the end of it – swollen in size and red in the face with her effort! When the last layer had been zipped up, they waddled into the living-room.

'All set?' Steve Bailey asked.

'All set,' Bart repeated.

'Then, let's go. Adam? Emily? Irene . . . are you coming? Let's party!'

There were several people down on the beach already. Mandy could see an assortment of brightly-coloured jackets and hats from the top of the hill. Bart had brought his sled, and they rode down together, leaving the adults to walk.

Mandy was introduced to many of the Baileys' friends. She struggled to remember all the different names, but at last she spotted some people she already knew: Dale and Michelle Rogers, Mr Ross, and the fisherman who had come to the door with the herring for the seals.

Mandy's dad was shaking a big bag of charcoal into the grate of the barbecue that Mr Rogers had helped to set up. He prodded the chunks of coal into a neat layer with a pair of tongs and set them alight. A plume of smoke rose into the air.

'That'll do nicely,' said Mr Hope, and he went over to help build the large driftwood fire. The scene reminded Mandy of bonfire night; everyone got involved with dragging bits of wood across the beach and piling them into a pyramid. Some of the smaller children ran around collecting up twigs and sticks, and threw them on to the top.

It was Dale Rogers who pronounced the pyre was complete. He struck a match to the wood at the base, and the flame caught and crackled, casting an immediate warm orange glow. There were shrieks of excitement as the blaze burned higher. Mandy huddled as close as she could, enjoying the sudden warmth.

But there was work to be done. Irene Bailey and Mrs Hope handed out large, black bin liners. The crowd began to break up, combing the beach from the farthest corners and walking towards the centre. Mandy could see people bending to pick up pieces of strewn and scattered litter, and drop them into their bags. Within just a few minutes, she found several fish hooks, the rusted lid of a tin can, an empty plastic bottle, and some fishing twine. Far from the fire, Mandy kept warm by bending and stuffing one piece of rubbish after another into her bin liner.

Mandy's thoughts turned to Melody and Harmony. She wondered just how the pair would cope out in the open seas. Lost in anxious thought, something caught her eye and she stared out across the pack ice. In a channel of grey water, she saw a number of dark, shiny heads. The seals slithered up on to the icy platforms and dived into the sea, sleek and swift. It was an encouraging sign – maybe Melody and Harmony would not be left behind after all.

'This is an enthusiastic turn-out,' Dale Rogers

remarked, passing Mandy with a bottle in his hand. 'Perhaps we will start a trend for beach cleaning all along this coast.'

'I hope so,' said Mandy. She walked over to her dad, who was setting out neat little rows of sausages on the grid. 'Dad!' she called. 'More seals – look!'

Adam Hope peered out across the pack ice, to where Mandy pointed. 'Ah, that's a wonderful sign,' he said. 'The migration's not over yet. There'll be more to come then, surely.'

Mandy nodded, her spirits soaring. More seals to look after Harmony and Melody!

At last daylight began to fade. Sleet started to fall, slowly at first, then more persistently, and small pieces of ice stung Mandy's cheeks. The litter collectors gathered around the burning logs, proudly displaying their bulging bin bags. Mrs Bailey and Mandy's mum, with Steve Bailey and Bart, handed round a large platter full of buttered buns, stuffed with crispy sausages, hamburgers and vegetarian burgers. Michelle Rogers followed them round with a big bottle of ketchup. Everyone had worked up an appetite in the bitter cold, and there were murmurs of satisfaction as the hot food was received. It wasn't long before Adam Hope announced that they had eaten every morsel.

'Let's set off home now – we'll meet back at our house.' Irene Bailey raised her voice so that everyone could hear her. 'We all deserve a glass of warm cider and some chocolate fudge brownies!'

There was a murmur of approval and smiles all round, as the crowd began to wander off towards the base of the big hill, lugging their bags along with them. Bart and Mandy put theirs on the green sled and began the trudge uphill, tugging on the rope just as they had with the seals.

Halfway up, they paused for breath, and Mandy turned to look back down at the beach. 'What a difference!' she exclaimed.

'We did a great job,' Bart agreed.

The crescent of beach was pristine. There were no tin cans or ripped black bin liners visible now. No wild bird or seal pup would come to harm on this beach, for a while at least.

Mandy grinned at Bart. 'Come on,' she said. 'I want a chocolate fudge brownie.'

The Baileys' small house was soon full to bursting. Emily Hope brought in a tray laden with jugs of warm apple cider and glasses were raised in a toast to a job well done.

Mandy looked around at the cheery faces crowded into the cosy room. Beyond the sitting room, through the picture window, dusk had fallen, giving the vast spread of ice a grey and ghostly look. She sat with her back to the fire, on the floor, and ate her third brownie.

Bart found his way to her side. 'Shall we go and see the pups?' he suggested.

She nodded and stood up. 'You get the flashlight,' she said. 'I'll get a bit of fish.'

It was completely dark, and so cold that it hurt to take a breath. They crunched over the snow to where Melody and Harmony lay together. The pups were dozing, tucked against one wall of the bunker. They looked round interestedly at the sound of Mandy and Bart's approach.

'Hi, there,' Bart said softly. Harmony gave a joyful bark and made towards Mandy. She stepped back, and tossed her a piece of fish. Melody focused on the fish tail in Bart's hand. He threw it and she leaped and caught it in mid-air. She landed on the ice with a rubbery slap.

'They're both so well, now,' Bart said, playing

the beam of light from the torch on the seals.

'Really well,' Mandy agreed. She knew there was no longer any worry about the health of the two pups. But their successful return to the ocean was another matter altogether. All she could do now was hope . . .

Mandy was up early the next morning. She slipped into the sitting room and found the binoculars. Scanning the sweep of frozen sea, she soon found

what she was looking for – another Harp seal group making the journey south. Her heart leaped with excitement. They were clearly visible, their dark heads bobbing like corks in the channels of water between the floes of ice.

'Ready to have another go?' Mandy's mum had come into the room, treading quietly on bare feet. 'Dad and I will go with you. We'll leave Irene and Steve to have a lie-in this morning, shall we?'

Mandy nodded. It had been late when yesterday's guests had finally gone, and then there had been the clearing-up to do. But everyone agreed it had been a wonderful party, and the whole community seemed to be united in a desire to keep the beach clean from now on.

Bart was awake and, as Mandy tiptoed past his room, she whispered that they were going down to the beach early, to take Melody and Harmony out to join the group of Harp seals on the ice floes. Then she went into her own room to get dressed.

Adam Hope backed up the truck and let down the back flap. The seal pups were put into their blankets and carried outside for yet another journey to the beach. Bart and Mandy climbed on board to hold them.

'Do you think they'll go this time?' Bart asked her, huddling into the hood of his anorak.

'I really hope so,' she said seriously. 'They can't stay here. And I'll be leaving soon,' she added. 'So I won't be able to help you look after them.'

Adam Hope steered the truck on to the beach, and he and Mandy's mum jumped out. They lifted first Harmony, then Melody on to the shore. Mandy peeled back the blankets. The two seals looked bewildered and excited, blinking their black eyes and looking around them. They lifted their heads as they breathed in the familiar scent of ice and ocean. Mandy silently willed the seals to follow their instincts – and go back to the sea.

'Go on,' Adam Hope urged. 'Off you go . . .'

Mrs Hope tossed a bit of fish out on to the closest ice shelf. Harmony launched herself after it, like a dog after a ball. Mandy saw her small head bob up and down in the water. Then the seal hauled herself out and heaved up on to the pack ice. Emily Hope lobbed another bit, and the herring slipped along, far across the pack ice. Melody's flippers began to work as she waddled after Harmony, as fast as she could go. Soon, both seals were sitting side by side on the ice shelf, looking around them hesitantly, as though wondering what to do next.

Mandy crossed her fingers. She felt hopeful, yet sad.

'Uh-oh,' Bart groaned. 'Melody's not sure at all . . .' The seal had turned around to face the gathering on the shore.

Adam Hope flapped his arms at her. 'Go on! Keep going!' he called.

'Oh! Look!' Mandy breathed. A large seal had suddenly appeared on the ice, slithering up from the channel of the water on the other side. It barked and approached the pair. Harmony lowered her head and submitted to the examination of the strange seal. They touched noses. Then another seal leaped out of the water and on to the ice, and another, until Melody and Harmony were surrounded.

Mandy lost sight of them for a moment, and she held her breath. 'They won't be harmed, will they?' she asked.

'No, I shouldn't think so,' Emily Hope said.

Adam Hope passed Mandy the binoculars. She caught a glimpse of Melody, in the middle of a crush of swirling seal bodies, looking back towards her with a wistful expression in her eyes. For an instant, Mandy was certain the seal pup would head straight back to her, closely followed by Harmony.

But she was wrong. As she passed the glasses to Bart, she saw Melody plunge like an arrow into the depths of the far channel. Harmony dived after her. The group of Harp seals slipped over the sides of the ice in pursuit.

'Wow,' Mandy said softly. 'They've gone. They've really gone.' She looked at Bart, who nodded slowly, his eyes trained on the spot where the seals had vanished.

'Good for them,' he said.

'Yes,' said Adam Hope. 'It was a job well done.'

'They've got a long, long journey ahead of them,' Mrs Hope reflected. They all stood, staring out across the ice, until Mandy had to blink against the glare and rub her eyes.

'We'd better head back. I've got to go to school,' Bart reminded them. But still he stayed where he was, watching the spot where they had last seen the seals.

'Yes,' Emily Hope acknowledged. She and Mr Hope turned and began to walk back to the truck, taking the blankets with them.

Mandy stood with Bart for a moment longer. She was just about to turn away when she spotted a pair of bobbing heads. Four black eyes gazed back at them from the channel of water closest to the shore.

'There they are!' yelled Bart. 'They've come to say goodbye.'

'Bye Harmony. Bye Melody,' Mandy called. 'Take care!'

One after the other, the seals dived beneath the surface of the ocean, and were gone.